Broken Mirrors

Marie McWilliams

Veranda Kuhar Studios
"Broken Mirrors"
Copyright © Marie McWilliams
Cover art: Veranda Kuhar
Editor: Richard MacNeill
Verandakuharstudios.com

For my Family.
Everything I do, I do for you.

Acknowledgements

First and foremost, I would like to thank Veranda Kuhar and Richard MacNeill of Veranda Kuhar Studios, without whom this book literally would not exist. Thank you for taking a chance on me and for your amazing work. Thank you to my Husband Chris, who patiently read everything I stuck under his nose, and who has always supported me. Thank you for my sister, one of my first readers and my biggest fan- you helped me believe in myself. Thank you to Sarah Jane, my dearest friend - your constant support, amazing advice and words of encouragement have meant the world to me. Thank you to my parents and my friends for supporting and encouraging me, particularly Paul and Susan whose professional advice was invaluable. Last but definitely not least, thank you to my perfect daughter, whose very existence inspires me to push myself to be a person she can be proud to call mum.

Chapter One
Present Day

Marie stared out of the small window while she waited for the officer to arrive for their appointment. It was a dull, rainy day and the weather seemed to reflect her mood. Every six to eight months or so over the past four years, she had stood in this same position, staring out this same window, waiting for whichever new officer they appointed to her husband's case. It always seemed to rain.

The door opened behind her and she heard a man with a thick Scottish accent apologize for being late. She didn't turn around immediately, and instead watched him in the reflection of the window while he adjusted the messy pile of papers he had brought with him and set down a paper cup containing what she could smell was cheap vending machine coffee. He was younger than the others had been, perhaps mid-thirties, and distinctly scruffier. He had longish, brown hair with a slight curl, stubble which must have taken at least a couple of days to cultivate, and he was wearing a pale blue shirt with the top button undone. He was handsome. His image took her by surprise; she was used to balding, chubby, middle aged men who sweat profusely and wore cheap, striped ties.

"Please, take a seat Mrs. Carter."

She pulled the heavy chair out from the table, as far as the chains connecting it to the floor would allow, and sat down directly facing the detective. She wondered how many times a chair had been thrown before they felt the chains were necessary. He continued to shuffle through the papers on the desk, yet to make eye contact with her. She took the time to appraise him, like a competitor assessing her opponent. She knew what was to come. He seemed relaxed, and confident. Again, this surprised her. Marie was used to making men nervous, particularly police officers. It had become habit to make them uncomfortable, to make them squirm. She saw it as their reward for hauling her in here over and over again, wasting her time. But, there was something different about him, something inexplicable which made him stand apart from the other detectives she'd encountered over the years.

After what seemed like several minutes, he looked up from the papers and stared at her. He had grey, blue eyes that matched the drizzly day outside, and he wore a friendly, half smile. He's attractive, for a peeler, she thought, as she stared right back at him. It continued like this for a few seconds, with each expecting the other to break eye contact first, something Marie was not used to, but she played along nonetheless, too stubborn to look away. Eventually, he glanced towards the clock behind her, and she felt pleased she'd obtained a small victory so early on in the game.

"Would you like a cup of tea or coffee?" he said, motioning towards the paper cup filled with an unappetizing looking fluid.

"No thank you, I would just like to get this over with."

"Have you got somewhere to be, Mrs. Carter?"

"To be honest, Detective...?"

"Detective Duncan, but please call me Fraser."

"To be honest, Detective Duncan, I would rather be anywhere than this place, so if you could just ask your questions."

He appeared to be a mildly amused, which just irritated Marie further.

"Well, I'm terribly sorry to be taking up so much of your valuable time, however I assure you, it's for a very good reason." He had that half smile again. I know exactly why I am here, she thought, and I know exactly what you want me to do. You want me to betray him. "I was hoping that we could get to know each other a little better, Mrs. Carter, but since you are so impatient, I guess we will just get right to it. Tell me about your husband."

Typical, they always lead with that. The question was so infuriatingly vague. What exactly about my husband are you curious about? His inside leg measurement? His drink of choice? How he liked to fuck? "What specifically would you like to know, detective?" she said, trying not to roll her eyes.

"Well, let's start at the beginning. How did you two meet?"

"Five years ago, at the club he owns, Capone's." A memory floated briefly into her mind. A handsome man in a suit, champagne, a goodnight kiss. As quickly as it came it was gone again.

"And how long have you been married now?"

"Three years." She hated these banal background questions. They had all of this information stored in their computers and in the bland coloured paper folders they insisted on carrying around all the time, as if they were trying to look busy.

"You're from Belfast, is that correct?"

"Yes."

"And when did you move here?"

"Just over five years ago."

"Why?"

Why? They had never asked that question before; it seemed so abrupt. She was briefly taken aback, unsure how to answer. Why? An abusive father, an emotionally absent mother, a desperation to escape my poor, bigoted neighbourhood, a chance at a better life, excitement. I wouldn't even know where to begin. "I wanted a fresh start." She had no intentions of telling this stranger her life story. She got the sense he knew not to push the point any further; he seemed unusually perceptive. Empathetic even.

"What does your husband do for a living?"

"He is in trading and acquisitions, antiques mostly. I do not help him with his work, nor do I know anything about it. If you want to know details, I suggest you ask him." She had that same feeling of déjà vu she got during these little "meetings", and wondered how many times she had uttered this same sentence before.

"That's one way of putting it, Mrs. Carter. Another way would be that he is a criminal, a gangster. A... murderer."

"My husband has never been prosecuted for any criminal offences detective. He has never had so much as a parking ticket, and for that matter...."

He interrupted her, "That doesn't prove he isn't what I say he is, Mrs. Carter."

She snapped, "Proof is something you don't have detective, isn't that what this little fishing expedition is all about?" She was getting angry now. They had never been so forward about it before, so cocky about the whole thing. She was used to a dance, a game, not this bull in a china shop routine. He reached over to the pile of papers, choosing a brown folder, and pulled out a crime scene photograph. It was a man, or at least what used to be a man. He was covered in blood and had multiple gaping wounds all over his bare chest, including a rather large and fatal looking one directly across his throat. Marie gagged, she couldn't help it. She had only seen something like that in the horror movies her sister had made her watch as a child, through fingers and from behind pillows. But they didn't compare to this; it was his eyes. Those staring, dead eyes that conveyed only one thing –terror.

"Mark Smith, thirty-five years old, father of two boys, eight and five years of age. Husband, son."

Before she could gather herself, he pulled out another photograph. This time it was a body without a head, the white of the spinal cord unmistakable against the bright red blood. "Paul Black, twenty-nine years old, father of none but a brother to two, a husband, son."

Again, another was removed from the folder, this time she couldn't look. She pushed the photographs away and stood up, walking over to the window, using the ledge to steady herself.

He continued despite her absence from the table. "Michael Williams, thirty-three years old, father of three children, all under the age of ten."

She heard the rustle of a crisp page being removed from the folder, and slammed onto the desk behind her. "Rodger Mathews, forty years old, father of one child, a six-month old baby. A husband and son." And again. He was yelling now. "Richard Davis, twenty-two years old." And again. "David Whyte, twenty-six years old."

"Stop it." she said, quieter than she had meant to. She was upset, and desperately trying not to show it.

Again, "Peter Adair, thirty...."

She turned to face him, tears welling up in her eyes, "Please stop." She shouted it this time.

He was standing now, the coffee, spilled on the desk in front of him, narrowly missing the stack of papers. He looked at her, and put the folder on the table. "Do you know what all these men had in common Mrs. Carter?" He spoke quietly, deliberately, "Your husband. I told you this was all for a good reason, and I meant it. I want to stop this from happening."

They stood in silence for what seemed like a lifetime, just staring at each other, both trying to compose themselves, both trying to read each other.

"Marie," he said, softly. This was new, they never called her by her first name, and it just unsettled her further. He continued, "I know you don't know anything about these murders. I know you don't really know what your husband does. I just want to show you what kind of man he really is, what he is capable of. I didn't want to upset you."

It was at this point she realized she was crying, a single tear cutting a warm line down the length of her face. He stepped toward her and handed her a white handkerchief. She didn't know how to react. These interviews had never gone like this before. She took the handkerchief from him, noticing the embroidered initials GD. She wondered who they referred to. You knew, she thought, You've always known.

"I need your help Marie. You can stop this from happening if you help me. We can protect you."

That expression, that same fucking phrase. It was as if something had just hit her in the chest, and brought her back into the room. This was the same game, the same dance, it was just that Detective Duncan had changed the rules.

"Protection?" she said through slightly gritted teeth, "I don't need your fucking protection." She looked at him directly in the eyes for the first time since before the photographs. She could see he knew he had lost her.

The interview room door opened behind him and a chubby, red faced, middle aged man wearing a mismatched stripy tie and shirt half entered the room. "Is everything OK in here? I heard shouting."

Marie smirked when she spotted the half-eaten doughnut in his hand. "Everything is fine," she said, "I think we are all done here, right detective?" She looked at him, steady now, once again in complete control.

"Right." He sounded disappointed, but there was something else in his tone – concern. He sounded concerned. Regardless, she wasn't going to spend a second longer in this place.

She walked back to the table and lifted her handbag, now dripping from the coffee which had pooled beneath it. She didn't care, she just wanted out of there. He moved to the door, catching it as it was shut by the other officer leaving, and held it open for her. Just as she walked out, he placed his free hand on her arm, so gently it sent a slight shiver throughout her body. She paused in the doorway, without really knowing why, and he leaned towards her so she could smell a mixture of cheap coffee and cigarettes on his breathe. "Take my card," he said, producing one from his shirt pocket, "It's not for if you change your mind. I doubt you will. It's just in case."

"In case what?"

"Just...in case."

She looked into his eyes, and saw it there again; concern. She took the card, although she wasn't sure why.

When she stepped out of the station, it was still raining, and the air was muggy and oppressive. She had never wanted to go home so badly. Her driver came running towards her, holding an umbrella and walked her to the car. She was so preoccupied with getting the hell away from the station that she didn't notice Detective Duncan watching her from that same, small interview room window, with that same concerned expression.

Chapter Two
-Five Years Ago

The shoes landed with a dull thud beside the Ikea sofa, which also doubled as Marie's bed. Despite the fact that it was too small and extremely uncomfortable, it was the current centre of her universe. She felt safe there, sheltered. It was where she ended up after pulling a double at the cafe, after fighting her way through the London Underground and streets full of unfriendly faces. It was her home.

"Wear those, you'll look great!"

Marie leant down and picked up the pair of cheap High Street heels, staring at her reflection in the glossy pleather. She looked tired and unkempt. She was tired and unkempt. She didn't want to go out to a bar, she wanted to curl up on her sofa and fall asleep to Father Ted reruns on Channel Four.

The shoes and the voice belonged to Sara, her cousin and the only person she knew in London. When Marie had escaped Belfast just a few months ago, Sara had not even hesitated when she asked her for a place to stay. She'd provided shelter, food, and a shoulder to cry on when it dawned on Marie that the London she envisioned in her head didn't really exist. She loved Sara; she owed her everything. So, she would put on some make-up and wear the cheap shoes and go to some bar so Sara could flirt and dance because that's what she wanted to do. That's what would make her happy. She dragged herself away from her sofa and made her way to the small bathroom they shared at the end of the hall.

She didn't have time to wash her hair, so she sprayed it with dry shampoo and put it up in a kind of bee hive. It was her fall back hair style, which she perfected over years of rushed plans and desperation to get out of her family home as quickly as possible. She fished through her make-up case, pulling out the ingredients necessary to make the bags under her eyes disappear and colour her skin, which over time had become sallow and almost sickly looking. When she was done, she took a step back and stared at the girl looking out at her. Marie was no model, but she was attractive in her own way. She had long, jet black hair, pale, porcelain skin, and bright, intelligent, blue eyes. Her grandmother had always told her she was a true Celt. She sighed heavily. She missed her grandmother deeply. As a child, whenever things became unbearable at home, she provided welcome distraction and kind words. Marie recalled when, at age seven, she had come home crying because she didn't look like the other pretty, blonde girls at school who made fun of her pale skin and cheap clothes, her grandmother had taken her to her bedroom and stood her in front of a mirror just like this one.

"Sure, why would you want to look like those girls anyway?" She had said, wiping away the tears, "Those girls all look exactly like each other, just like everybody else. You, you're special." She had taken out an old shoe box, containing dozens of black and white photographs, and after a quick shuffle removed a small square one with crumpled edges. "That's me." Marie took the picture from her and stared at it in awe. Although the girl in the photo was a little older, perhaps ten or eleven years old, the resemblance was unmistakable. Same eyes, same hair, same skin. "You are what they call a classic beauty my love, like Audrey Hepburn and Bettie Page."

Marie didn't know who those people were, but she knew her grandmother was the most wonderful person in the world. She was beautiful and kind, and she looked just like her, and that made her happier than she had ever felt before. Her grandmother had always been the anchor that held her family firm, and when she had passed away days before Marie's tenth birthday, what remained floated out to sea and became lost in the fog forever.

The sudden thump on the door dragged Marie back from her memories. She wasn't sure how long she had been standing there.

"Are you done in there yet? I need to get ready too, for fuck sake."

Marie apologized to the blur of red hair rushing past her into the bathroom, getting only a grunt in response before the door slammed shut. Making her way back to her sofa, she stopped briefly at the navy suitcase on the living room floor and fished out a black body con dress. It was Marie's best, a bargain in a sale a few years before. It hugged her slender frame in all the right places and made her feel like she was Bettie Page. She grabbed Sara's shoes, abandoned earlier on the floor, and surveyed herself in the full length mirror leaning against the living room wall. Not bad, she thought, straightening the skirt. She noticed two glasses on the small table where they ate their meals, one full and the other empty, and sniffed at the full one before taking a sip. It was Vodka and Diet Coke, although it was obvious Sara had liberally applied the vodka as she always did. She called them 'Sara measures' and they were lethal. She took a few gulps, her face crumpling under the sheer strength of the drink, and instantly felt more relaxed. She applied a thick coat of red lipstick, which she found lurking at the bottom of her giant handbag, and taking another glance in the mirror behind her, she suddenly felt up for a night out. She felt good, and looked good. And why not? You work hard enough...you deserve to relax and have fun.

Marie didn't know where they were going, nor did she ask. London still felt so foreign to her. She constantly carried around the fear that she might get lost, that she could simply take a wrong turn one day and disappear forever. After about twenty minutes, the black taxi turned into a darkened side street and stopped outside an innocuous looking Victorian building. As Sara paid the driver, Marie surveyed the place, trying to get a feel for what lay ahead. The building looked old fashioned, and appeared to have been converted at some point into a bar. Marie wondered what its original purpose had been. There was no sign, apart from a small, shiny brass plaque beside the door which read Capone's. In fact, it was so understated that if the large, bald man wearing a black jacket and ear piece had not been standing by a velvet rope outside the entrance, one would simply have walked by. It intrigued her.

"What is this place?" She turned to face Sara, just as the taxi pulled away.

Sara was a beautiful girl. She was tall and slim, with long, auburn hair and chocolate brown eyes. The problem was, she wore a thick caked on layer of make-up and garish, brightly coloured mini dresses which barely maintained her dignity. Sara had always dressed the way she thought men wanted her to look, to please them, not to suit herself. In truth, it made Marie feel a little sorry for her.

"It's this place my mate was telling me about. It's ridiculously exclusive, and a lot of rich guys come here to meet pretty girls. But he knows the staff 'cause he delivers the booze for the bar; he's got our names on the list."

Marie suddenly felt a little disheartened. Sara's only focus in life seemed to be to meet a suitable mate, preferably a rich one. She had visions of herself sitting alone at a bar after Sara had disappeared with some greasy man; ditched once again. But what could she do? She owed Sara big time, and besides, she was here now and her curiosity had been piqued. She might as well see what lay beyond the front door of this unassuming little building.

They approached the bouncer with trepidation. It wasn't the first time Sara's 'mates' had failed to deliver on their promises.

"Name?" His East End voice was deep and gruff and matched his appearance perfectly. Marie noticed raw cuts and swelling on the knuckles of his right hand and wondered what that particular patron had done to warrant such force.

"Grant," Sara said, surreptitiously grabbing Marie's arm and moving her closer, "Plus one."

Grant? Marie rolled her eyes. Why was she surprised? It wasn't the first time Sara had given a fake name, choosing one she deemed more glamorous than her own. The last time it had been Monroe. She wondered what was wrong with McMaster anyway.

The bouncer did not have a clip board, and instead peered up to a small camera mounted above the entrance. He placed two fingers over his ear piece, and with the other hand lifted a small microphone clipped to his jacket, bringing it closer to his lips. "Grant plus one?"

The action reminded Marie of CIA operatives in Hollywood movies, and she couldn't help but smile at the thought.

After a short pause, he made a sharp nod at the camera before lifting the velvet rope off the polished brass stand and ushering them inside. For a second, Marie felt like a VIP or celebrity, and then almost instantly blushed at her foolishness. For all she knew, inside was a seedy strip bar or a miserable little pub filled with sleazy old men. It was, however, neither.

A short hallway led to two large etched glass interior doors with sweeping, polished brass handles. They depicted a 1920s style figure of a woman, in draped clothing, who seemed to be dancing to the muffled music coming from behind them. Marie thought it was one of the most beautiful things she had ever seen. She eagerly opened the doors and was stunned by just how beautiful the bar within really was. There was a large, crystal drop chandelier hanging in the centre of the domed roof, pouring warm, golden light into the room below. It had dark wood panelling lining the walls, broken up by brass Art Deco wall-mounted lights and oil paintings of more beautiful women, some dancing and others simply staring out at you.

At present, both women stood on marble steps with brass bannisters. One could choose to stay on this upper level which encircled the outskirts of the room and was dotted with small round tables with red, velvet tablecloths and gold backed chairs. The lower level consisted of a large bar to the right, made of the same dark wood panelling. Behind the bar was mirrored, and glass bottles of every colour stood on invisible shelves. Marie was unaware so many types of alcohol even existed. There were small red glass lamps at intervals along the polished bar top, which bathed those waiting to buy drinks in an eerie light. To the left were a handful of booths, deliberately placed in shadow, giving those within the privacy they clearly coveted. And in the centre was a large open space where a half dozen people currently danced along to the music, lined at either side with more of those little red velvet tables.

Directly ahead lay a small stage, with brass spotlights framed by red velvet curtains. The six-piece band was playing jazz music which Marie didn't know, but instantly loved. They wore tuxedos, apart from the singer. She was a tall, slim woman of about thirty with long, fiery red hair in a 50s style wave. She wore a floor length white beaded dress, which caught the light as she swayed to the music, singing into an old fashioned microphone, sending millions of little light beams bouncing along the walls around her. She was breathtaking.

Marie stood a moment, simply drinking it in. She felt as if she had stepped back in time. Perhaps those etched glass doors had been a portal, a gateway into the past. It reminded her of the speakeasies in the black and white movies she had watched with her grandmother as a child, and she instantly fell in love with it.

"It's a bit old fashioned, isn't it?"

Marie just stared at Sara, whose face plainly showed her dislike of the place. They were polar opposites, disagreeing on almost everything, with only their familial blood connecting them in any way. Marie had often wondered if, had they not been family, they would have ever been friends at all. She shook the thought from her mind. "I think it's wonderful."

"You would! Come on, I definitely need a drink."

They made their way to the bar, weaving in and out of people. It was very busy, and the chatter of those around them was almost as loud as the music. Marie made a beeline for two empty stools at the bar and sat down in expectation of a long wait. There were at least a dozen people vying for the attention of the lone barman. She lifted a small leather book, which contained dozens of unfamiliar cocktails and drinks as well as the wines, beers, and champagnes on offer. There were no prices, and Marie had learned early on that in London, that was code for expensive.

"What can I get you?"

Marie looked up, surprised. A man of about twenty-five, wearing a friendly smile and a black pork pie hat, was watching her. She didn't know what she wanted. She didn't know what she could afford. She looked to Sara for some guidance, only to discover she was already in deep conversation with a handsome, silver haired man, laughing at his jokes and placing her hand on his arm at every opportunity. Already? She looked back towards the barman, suddenly feeling extremely alone.

He seemed to sense what was wrong, and leaned closer to her. "The Moscow Mule is our special today; it's only a fiver." He winked at her.

Marie nodded, getting the distinct impression that this special offer was exclusive to her. She had no idea what a Moscow Mule was, but she definitely needed a drink and she was grateful for his kindness.

While he clinked glasses and crushed ice, she turned her focus to the people rather than the setting, pretending not to notice Sara making her way to one of the booths with her new friend. It was an eclectic mix. There were men in expensive looking dark suits wearing gold watches and talking to beautiful women draped in diamonds next to men in cheap looking black jackets and jeans laughing loudly with each other or chatting up women in tight mini dresses. Marie got the distinct impression these women were prostitutes, but she couldn't explain why she thought so. It was a strange mix of people, and few of them seemed to fit the glamorous, old time surroundings. The thing that screamed out to Marie the most was that none of them were on their own. Everyone was in large groups, or couples, talking and laughing with one another, except for her. She was sitting alone at the bar, and in that moment, surrounded by all those people, she felt incredibly lonely. This feeling wasn't new to her, of course. Even when she had been home in Belfast with her family, she still felt alone, and that feeling had only heightened since her arrival in London. Marie had always felt like she was on the outside of everything, looking in; an observer, choosing to watch rather than participate.

"Here you go, my world famous Moscow Mule."

Marie started. She was so lost in thought that she hadn't even noticed the barman approach. "Thank you, really," she said as she passed him the money. He smiled that same sympathetic smile, before moving on to the next customer. She took a sip, and was instantly warmed by the strong taste of ginger and vodka. She smiled and felt herself relax slightly.

It was then she noticed the man at the other end of the bar. He was in his early thirties, with brown hair and striking ice blue eyes. He was wearing a dark navy suit, with a blue tie which mirrored those eyes, and a blue polka dot pocket square, perfectly embodying the vintage yet stylish quality of his surroundings. There were three things that made him instantly distinguish himself from all the others around her. Firstly, out of the crowds and couples, groups and packs, he was the only other person there alone. Unlike Marie, however, it was clear this did not bother him in the slightest. He looked incredibly sure of himself and completely at ease. Secondly, he was uncommonly handsome, strikingly so. The word that leapt into Marie's mind was sexy. Finally, and most importantly, he was staring right at her. Of all the women in the room, from the diamond clad stunners to the tacky yet pretty young things, he was staring at her, and she wasn't sure why. She felt those glacial eyes burning holes deep into her body until the heat rose to her cheeks and she blushed like a little girl. She looked away from him, suddenly feeling embarrassed and self-conscious.

She wished she was more confident, more like Sara, able to talk to men she found attractive; to flirt and seduce. But that wasn't Marie. She knew herself, knew her own mind, but she wasn't brave about it. She always knew what she wanted to say, but lacked the confidence to say it, and as a result had always held herself back from reaching her full potential. She was angry with herself for being so timid; London was supposed to be a new start, a new more self-assured Marie. She looked towards the end of the bar, hoping his obvious interest in her might increase her confidence, but he was gone, the space where he had been now filled with a rather drunken looking blonde woman frantically waving at the barman. You missed your chance.

"Can I buy you a drink?" The voice came from behind her and caught her off guard. She was filled with a mixture of excitement and trepidation, causing a distinct queasiness deep in the pit of her stomach as she turned to face a completely different man. She felt instantaneous and overwhelming disappointment. The man in front of her was not an unattractive man. He looked to be in his mid-twenties and had styled, dirty fair hair and blue eyes. He clearly worked out, as was obvious through the one size too small Armani shirt he was wearing, and he clearly had money, based on the silver Rolex watch on his left wrist. To Marie, he smacked of style over substance however, and she was not interested. Perhaps on another night, she may have flirted with him to get a free drink and to have bolstered her low self-confidence slightly, but it would never have gone further than that. And after that brief heart pounding moment with her mystery man, she was definitely not in the mood for wasting her time on someone she considered second rate in comparison.

"No thank you," she said, as she turned towards the bar, making what she thought was a universal gesture for I'm not interested in sleeping with you. Go away. However, that message was clearly lost in translation, and he sidled up to her, squeezing into a narrow space amongst the other patrons to stand uncomfortably close to her. Marie was irritated; she hated cocky men. Confidence was attractive in a man, cockiness however was incredibly off putting, and that was a fine line this man had clearly failed to tread.

"You are far too beautiful to be drinking alone. Let me buy you a drink. We can be company for each other." Before Marie had a chance to respond, he had attracted the barman's attention, waving him over to them. "Another vodka coke and one of whatever she's having."

She. The inflection he put on that single word grated her further, and she began to lose patience. She opened her mouth in order to politely tell him to bugger off, when he beat her to the punch.

"My name's Aaron. And you are?"

"My name's Marie, look I....."

"Marie. That's a beautiful name for a beautiful girl." It was bad enough that he had interrupted her; she hated being interrupted. She thought it implied that the interrupter considered her opinions unimportant and insignificant. Not worth listening to. But as he spoke those cheesy words and smiled his sleazy smile, he placed his hand on her bare, upper thigh, squeezing firmly, making Marie feel immediately uncomfortable and suddenly exposed. She pushed his hand off her body, stood up from the stool, and went to walk away when he grabbed her wrist tightly, pulling her back onto it.

"Where do you think you're going to? We were getting to know each other, and I bought you a drink, so you owe me something."

Owe you? The initial shock of this action had left her feeling slightly afraid; but that sentence, once uttered, shattered any fear she had felt and replaced it with blind rage. Owe you? Marie may have been a little naive, and she may have lacked any and all self-belief at times, but she was not weak. She had watched her father hit her mother dozens of times over the years, and even as a child had felt a few of the blows herself, but she was not weak. She had seen her mother withdraw from the world, and she had vowed she would never be like her. She would never take it lying down, or become a victim.

A memory flashed into her mind of the last time her father had hit her. She was little, perhaps seven or eight years old, and she had broken something by accident. The object eluded her but the feeling of injustice had not; she knew she hadn't meant to break whatever it was. It was just an accident. She remembered screaming those words over and over – "It was an accident" – as the blows had rained down on her young body. She remembered being convinced that that was the moment she was going to die. That, at eight years old, her short life was over because of a simple accident. But that's when she heard the thud of something very hard hitting something, or someone, above her. She had looked up through her bruised arms and seen her grandmother holding a large piece of wood, retrieved from the ever increasing pile of litter outside their home, standing over the cowering figure of her father. "You touch that girl again and I'll kill you, you hear me? I don't give a fuck if you're my son, I'll murder you with my bare hands." Afterwards she had told her, "Don't you ever take that from anyone my love. You're worth so much more."

He never touched Marie again after that, or her mother. Her grandmother was the only person her father had ever shown any respect for, or any fear of, and she became Marie's protector after that day. Her hero. Her strength. Marie lost any connection to her family after she had died, and immediately began her countdown until she was old enough to leave them forever.

Owe you? Marie pulled her arm free from him and slapped him around the face, hard enough to leave the distinct impression of her fingers on his reddening right cheek. "Don't you fucking touch me. I don't owe you anything. Prick."

He seemed genuinely in shock. Clearly he was used to dealing with a very different breed of women. Women who were distracted by shiny watches and impressed by designer shirts and smooth lines. Marie was definitely not one of those girls.

She hadn't noticed her mystery admirer moving towards her side of the bar, nor did she notice now how he had signalled one of the larger patrons over and whispered instructions in his ear. She was so angered by the entire incident, in fact, that as she stormed towards the exit, weaving through amused looking onlookers, she did not notice this larger patron grabbing the man who still sat stunned at the bar, forcing him towards a side door.

She was so angry and upset, fighting back tears as she left. All she could think about was getting out of that bar and away from that man. She thought about Belfast, about how desperate she had been to leave, about how London was to be her salvation. A new start. A new her. But it was just the same old shit in a different city. She had escaped her family, yes, but she was still the same frightened little girl, no matter how much she told herself otherwise. She was angry with herself for being so naive.

She had almost reached the exit when, lost in thought, she walked straight into a member of the door staff, thudding into his large, overworked chest. She muttered an apology under her breath without even making eye contact and moved around his giant frame. He stopped her, placing his hand gently on her upper right arm.

"Miss, the owner would like a word with you, to apologize about what just happened."

She was surprised the owner gave a shit. "I'm fine, it's fine...." She was going to make a vague declaration about how 'these things happen' knowing full well that this was untrue. Being groped by some loathsome degenerate was definitely not fine, and it most certainly wasn't just one of those things, but she just wanted out of there.

"I couldn't disagree more, Miss…?"

She turned, half expecting a silver haired, tuxedo clad, older gent kind of owner, based on the style and theme of the bar. But standing before her, adjusting his silver cuff link, was the mystery man himself. She felt her heart stop momentarily, unsure what to do or say. He was even more handsome up close. He had a very short almost beard, ginger in colour, which she had not noticed from the other side of the bar, and a kind smile formed from two perfect lips. Marie thought about what those lips tasted like, and felt herself blush again. She hated how she would go all giddy and school girlish around a man she found attractive. She became suddenly and painfully aware that she had been staring at him for several seconds without saying something. "Uh McMaster, Marie McMaster. But please call me Marie."

"Well Marie, my name is Malcolm Carter. I own this establishment. I wanted to apologize for that Neanderthal. I don't tolerate such behaviour in my bars."

Bars plural? Incredibly handsome and a wealthy businessman; Sara would call him the motherlode. Marie smiled to herself at the thought. She didn't care about such things. All she cared about was that she was very attracted to him, and she knew straight away that if he asked her to go home with him tonight, she would.

"Thank you, Mark. That will be all."

She realised he was speaking to the mammoth bouncer behind her. She hadn't seen he was still standing there.

"Please, let me get you a drink to make up for what happened. I would hate for someone like that to have ruined your night and given you a bad impression of the place. After all, I would prefer it if you came back again in the future."

She looked at him as he directed her towards those darkened booths. By the way he looked at her, she could tell he found her just as attractive as she did him, and she felt her confidence increase instantly. As they passed the first one, a quick glance revealed Sara making out with the man from earlier. Marie had a slight urge to yell her name, to point out Malcolm to Sara so she could see how gorgeous he was, but she clearly had her hands full, and Marie didn't want to spoil this moment with her childish ideas. They arrived at the last booth, which was marked Private by another brass plaque. He offered her his hand as she stepped up and inside to the slightly raised seats, shuffling along, until she had a perfect view of the entire bar.

She searched for the man who started these events in motion, but he was nowhere to be seen. She assumed he had sidled off, embarrassed by her very public rejection, but she was mistaken. At that exact moment, unbeknownst to her, he was lying in the alleyway running along the side of the bar in a pool of his own blood and urine whilst three heavy set men kicked him over and over again, reigning painful, bone shattering blows all over his broken body. He would wake up two days later in a hospital with no memory of that evening's events, numerous shattered bones, missing teeth and bleeding on the brain. Marie would, a week later, recognise his picture in a small article, an appeal by the police for information, providing the Crime Stoppers telephone number. She would dismiss any connection between his fate and the events of that evening almost as quickly as the thought entered her head, but one day she would know exactly what happened to that man. She would know, and she would accept it, perhaps even approve of it. But that was all still to come.

While he was at the bar, she frantically sought out a compact mirror from inside her unnecessarily large and cluttered handbag. It was shaped like a gold clam shell, which opened to reveal a cracked mirror inside. It had belonged to her grandmother, one of the many tangible reminders she carried with her always. Her friends and family had told her to repair it or throw it away, but Marie preferred it this way, preferred it broken. It made the images within more real. Life wasn't perfect, and neither was she. They were just as cracked and damaged. She looked at the reflection, assessing herself – a dash of powder, a new application of the red lipstick and she felt a little more like herself again.

"I hope you like champagne."

She peered around the edge of her own reflection to see him standing there with a silver ice bucket in one hand and two champagne glasses in the other. "I love it."

Truthfully, she had only had it once at a family wedding and could not remember whether she liked it or not, having drunk so much that day that her memories were nothing but blurs and shadows.

He moved in beside her, sitting closer than required. She could smell his after shave; it was intoxicating. He poured them a glass each, and she took a sip, feeling the bubbles slide down her throat like liquid gold. Instantly she felt at ease for the first time that evening, something which she found unusual. People, particularly men, would be treated with suspicion and slight apprehension prior to earning her trust. But for some as yet undiscovered reason, she felt completely comfortable with Malcolm, despite only knowing him a matter of moments. She could sense almost immediately that he was different, and that, more than anything else, aroused her.

"Well Marie, tell me about yourself."

"There's nothing much to tell really. I grew up in Belfast and moved here a few months back. I work in a cafe and live with my cousin for the moment."

"I'm sure there's a lot more to you than that. What do you do for fun?"

Marie had one and only one escape; one which she had utilised often since childhood. "I read."

Books offered a new life, new worlds, an adventure. Pure, one hundred percent escapism, if only for a little while. When she was a child and she could hear her parents arguing or the broken glass and yelling of the riots outside, she would hide under her blankets with a book and a torch. Gulliver and Alice had been more real to her than any of her schoolmates, their worlds a welcome departure from her surroundings. When her father would hit her or her mother, she would pretend to herself that he was just like Jekyll and Hyde, that he had just taken his potion and wasn't really her father, he just looked like him. One day soon, he would change back. When her grandmother died, she pretended she had gone to Neverland, that Peter had simply whisked her through the stars and she was now taking care of the lost boys, exactly like she had taken care of her, that they simply needed her more.

"And what is your favourite book?"

"I love so many, but if I had to choose one it would be Wuthering Heights."

He smiled a wry smile, "Ah, Heathcliff. The villainous anti-hero. I always rather liked him. Do you like your men dark and wicked Marie?"

"I like my men passionate."

He smiled again, a smile Marie found incredibly warm and charming. "Speaking of passion, I was very impressed by how you handled that man at the bar. People who lack respect are far too common these days. I admire anyone who redresses that."

"Maybe it's the Northern Irish blood. Makes me feisty." She was trying to make light of the incident. The spotlight he was putting on her was something she was not accustomed to, and she wasn't sure how to react.

"You aren't used to compliments are you?" Holy shit! Did he just read my mind? He leaned in even closer, so that she could feel his breath on her neck, causing every hair on her body to stand up. "That's something I shall have to redress then."

He turned his eyes to look directly at her, and for a second she thought, she hoped, he would kiss her, but he sat straight again and took a sip of champagne, maintaining that gaze. Once again, she was aware that they were sitting in silence, except this time it didn't bother her.

"Do you like my bar?" He swept the hand holding the champagne glass, indicating the room around them. It brought her back to reality. Until that moment, she had forgotten their surroundings. The music and people had faded into the background like shadows, and she felt as if they were completely alone there; like they were the only people in existence.

"I do. Very much. It reminds me of the old black and white movies I used to watch with my grandmother when I was little. Like I've stepped back in time."

"I prefer the past in many ways. I think they had more style, as well as more substance; more respect. This is my way of keeping that alive, I suppose."

Marie thought he looked sad for a second, but he was soon smiling at her again and whatever thought had crossed his mind had clearly passed.

"I've definitely not seen you here before. I know I would remember you."

She felt the colour rise to her cheeks, and she couldn't help smiling. She wanted to be cool and aloof, but her biology was betraying her. "My cousin heard about it from a mate; he got us on the list. She brought me with her."

"Where is your cousin?"

"She's around, trying her best to snag a rich boyfriend."

He laughed, a confident and bold laugh. He looked even more handsome when he laughed. "Well good luck to her." He raised his glass in a mock toast, making Marie laugh in return. He suddenly became serious again, holding her gaze. "I'm glad she brought you. I've had a hell of a day, and your company, your presence, has made it right again."

That blush made an appearance again. "What happened?"

"It's just my work. There was some unpleasantness."

"Oh dear. What do you do?"

He appeared to think about it, like he was searching for the right words. "I'm.... in trading and acquisitions, antiques mostly."

She knew he was telling a half truth. It sounded rehearsed, like he was reading it from a script, but she didn't care. They had only just met; she didn't expect his life story. All that mattered at that point was the fact that she wanted him, badly, and he clearly found her equally attractive. She wasn't imagining some budding romance, or expecting a relationship; she was a realist. She expected them to sleep together and probably never speak again, but she was okay with that. She was okay with that the moment she had seen him.

"Marie...." She loved the way he said her name. "Would you like to come home with me tonight?"

Chapter Three
-Present Day

By the time she arrived home, her emotions had not dissipated. If anything, they increased. She was angry. Angry with the detective for being so forward, for being so full on. Angry with herself for letting it get to her. But mostly, she was upset at those photographs, those images of things that were once living people, swimming around inside her head, appearing when she closed her eyes for too long. Why had it affected her so much?

Because they made it real. The door slammed behind her with a thundering bang which echoed around the entranceway, startling her. She was so preoccupied with her thoughts that she had no memory of being driven home or of opening the front door. She stopped still in the middle of the room, hoping he wasn't home. Malcolm would ask questions, he would want to know why she was upset and she knew where that could lead for the detective and his colleagues. She couldn't tell him, but she couldn't lie to him either. Sure, she had tried on occasion, but he was able to read every line on her face like an open book. He knew her better than she knew herself, and she couldn't hide anything from him. After several seconds, when he didn't appear, she breathed a sigh, only then realising that she was holding her breath.

She removed her fur coat and walked towards the kitchen. She didn't care what time of day it was, she needed a drink. A big one. Opening the wine cooler, she grabbed the first bottle that came to hand and poured herself a large glass. Only after gulping down half of it did she start to feel herself again.

She tried to organise her thoughts, to make sense of the day's events. Why had she reacted like that? She knew what her husband did for a living, she wasn't an idiot, but she had made her peace with it a long time ago, on the day she arrived home early from the Spa. The day she'd seen him 'working'. She had been faced with a choice that day, to leave and never come back or to stay and accept things as they were. She had chosen to stay. She stayed because she loved him too much to leave. She stayed because of everything they faced together, because he made the difficult choice to give up so much to be with her. But most of all, quite simply, she loved him so much it didn't matter what he did. The memory forced its way inside her mind, playing out like some awful Grind House movie. The pleading eyes of a man, the red of his blood, Malcolm's eerie calmness. It was like it happened yesterday. She thought of that day often in the past, but as time had gone on she thought about it less and less. Time has a funny way of helping us come to terms with any event, no matter how horrible. And the truth was, she never regretted her decision. Not once.

That memory however, was nothing compared to those photographs today. Those bodies, those mutilated people, it was like a story she chose to ignore or suspend in a dubious state of disbelief was now thrust headfirst into reality.

The truth was, she knew why she was upset. She was upset because she could no longer pretend she didn't know the full reality of the situation. She could no longer push it all to the empty space at the back of her mind and act as if it did not exist. She realised she had been like a child hiding under the covers to avoid the monsters around her, and that flimsy safety blanket had just been ripped away by Detective Duncan. She felt a flash of anger.

How dare he? What gave him the right? She knew deep down that he wasn't really to blame, that he had merely been doing his job, but it felt good to blame someone. She preferred to outwardly focus her anger at him, rather than inwardly at herself. We all do it, project because it's easier; it was just another example of hiding under her safety blanket.

She went to pour another glass, only then seeing the bottle was empty and about an hour had passed since she arrived home. She could feel she was drunk, her head felt heavy and her limbs clumsy and awkward. She wasn't too drunk however, to hide the bottle at the bottom of the recycling bin, and wash and replace the wine glass. Those awkward questions from a concerned husband could happen, and she still wasn't ready for that.

Gripping the banister tightly, she struggled upstairs to their bedroom and began to undress. She was sure a shower and some sleep would make everything go away. At least she hoped they would. The bedroom, like the rest of the house, was decorated in a perfect marriage of old and new styles. Modern art hung on white painted walls alongside classic, renaissance style oil paintings. Her industrial kitchen was in sharp contrast to the three small antique French chandeliers which hung above the kitchen island. But her favourite items around their home were the little bits and pieces they had acquired together on their travels around the world or from happy moments in their life together. The piece of driftwood they found on the beach in Cuba, the little antique silver gilt mirror which hung above the sink in their en suite bathroom, found in a little flea market in Paris, and the dried flowers under a bell jar in the upstairs hallway, taken from her wedding bouquet. She loved this house, it was her safe haven, her little piece of heaven in the centre of London.

When Marie thought of it as little however, she meant in comparison to the vastness of the heavens: their five-bedroom town house in Kensington was anything but small. It had been her wedding present from Malcolm. The day they married, they were supposed to go straight to the airport, but they instead arrived outside this house. He carried her over the threshold and they consummated their marriage on the floor of the entrance way, amongst boxes and painting sheets, too consumed with each other to make it any further inside. She smiled at the memory; this house had been a part of them from the moment they started their new life, and she adored every inch of it.

She stepped under the warm rushing water of the shower and let it pour over her body, washing away the morning's events. She watched the little black drops of eye liner and mascara run down her face in the reflection of the glass until the combination of the steam and wine made her feel dizzy. She didn't even dry off, instead falling onto their mahogany four post bed wrapped in a towel, her wet hair dripping onto the rug below.

She fell into a disturbed sleep quickly, dreaming she was following a bright white snake slithering through a large pool of red blood before transforming suddenly into a spinal cord, jerking around as if it were alive. It made her want to vomit. As she walked through the blood, she left bare footprints which stayed only a moment before the blood moved into them, making them disappear. She began to feel panic as the blood seemed to rise and fall like the waves of the ocean, threatening to wash her out to sea and drown her. She ran towards a black door, hoping it would be her salvation, her escape, but the door didn't lead to anywhere. It simply opened onto a large mirror, the reflection revealing the full extent of the bloody ocean, ever growing behind her, with herself in the middle. She was terrified. The image of herself appeared so calm, so contented, but she knew she was screaming; she could hear herself over the roar of the waves. Before she could do anything, the mirror suddenly shattered all around her, and that was the moment she woke up, drenched in sweat.

She took a minute to calm down, for a split second believing she was still in that place, and when the feeling passed, she remained haunted by the images and by her own fear. She looked around the room and noticed it was dark outside. Checking the time, she realised she'd been asleep for nearly five hours. She felt a chill. She was naked, the towel laying nearby, contorted and twisted.

She put on her dressing gown, a silk kimono she purchased on their trip to Japan, and checked her reflection in the mirror. She looked like shit, her face was puffy and flushed and she still had black make-up inking her face, but she was starting to feel a little better, the images from her nightmare fading like mist. She washed her face with ice cold water and checked her reflection again. She was beginning to look herself again.

She checked her phone; three missed calls from Malcolm. He would have been worrying about her when she didn't pick up. He always worried about her. Over the years, he had accumulated many enemies and all of them were a very real threat to Marie, simply because he loved her. She went to phone him back, wondering why he hadn't sent someone to check on her, as was usual. As if he heard her thoughts, the bedroom door opened and he was standing there.

"Are you okay? You didn't answer your phone or the land line. I was worried."

She hadn't heard either ring, her sleep so heavy. "I'm fine, I fell asleep that's all. I'm sorry."

He embraced her in a tight, comforting hug. It felt so wonderful being held by him, she forgot everything in that moment. She forgot, and she remembered. She remembered why she made the choices she made, she remembered how his love was worth every sacrifice, every compromise. "I began to imagine all sorts of horrific things happening to you.

I'm so glad you're okay."

"I'm fine, I'm fine! Stop worrying about me, I'm a big girl."

He released his hold just enough so he could look at her face, and for a split second, before he kissed her, she thought she saw fear in his eyes. She dismissed it instantly, Malcolm was never afraid. He was the bravest man she had ever known. But what did linger for a few moments was the thought that this level of concern was a dramatic increase on the norm. He worried yes, but at times like this, he would have sent an employee to check on her. This time, he had come personally. She knew there was something wrong, something with work, something big. She knew they had a new enemy, a new threat. A threat which he, her fearless husband, took far more seriously than the others. A threat which, unbeknownst to her, was watching them now. An enemy with a plan.

Chapter Four
-Five Years Ago

When Marie awoke that morning, she felt euphoric. There hadn't been a lot of conversation that night. In fact, immediately after arriving at his large loft apartment, they ripped each other's clothes off. It was the most amazing sex Marie had ever had. She looked at the space beside her where Malcolm had slept, where he laid holding her before going to shower. She could still smell him on her skin.

For the first time, she took stock of her surroundings. The bedroom was large with bare brick walls and paintings similar to those hung in the bar. The bed was a dark wood sleigh bed with a small bedside table and lamp, and the only other furniture in the room was a tweed patterned armchair in one corner next to a small pile of books and a large gilt mirror hanging opposite the bed. For a room with so little furnishings, it felt warm and welcoming. She felt comfortable and safe, which surprised her. She'd never gone home with a stranger for a one night stand before. She had casual sexual partners, but they were people she knew for a good while, friends with benefits, so to speak. She always considered a one night stand a dangerous prospect. The man could be anyone; a rapist, a murderer. She would never have risked it, even back home in Ireland. But there was something different about Malcolm, something she couldn't put her finger on. She felt like they'd known each other for years.

She fished her phone out of her hand bag and sat up with a start when she realised it was nearly two o'clock in the afternoon. How had she slept so long? Six missed calls from Sara; she would be going out of her mind with worry. Holding her phone to one ear with her shoulder, she began seeking out her various articles of clothing whilst simultaneously trying to hold the improvised sheet toga around her naked body. It was not easy.

"Where the hell are you? I was worried sick!!" She sounded more angry than concerned.

"I know, I know I'm sorry! I went home with this guy last night."

"What? You don't do that! You've never done that! Are you sure you're okay? If he is there and you can't speak say carrot! If you're in danger say carrot."

Marie laughed, "He's not here, you weirdo. I'm fine, he was just different, that's all."

Her tone suddenly shifted, and Marie thought she detected a hint of pride in her voice. "Really? Do tell!"

She went to speak, but then it dawned on her that she didn't really want to tell anyone. As stupid as it sounded, it had been such a wonderful evening, so personal to her, and she didn't want to spoil it by letting other people in. "What about that silver fox you were getting into? Did he take you home?"

"Oh, his name's Mark and he's a lawyer or a

barrister or something like that. He wants to take me to dinner tomorrow night. He had a Ferrari, Marie, a Ferrari! And a Rolex, so you know he's loaded!"

Her plan had worked – turn the subject around to Sara and she would forget her original line of questioning – she loved talking about herself. After a quick discussion about what she should wear to the date, Marie managed to get her off the phone. Her incessant talking was ruining her buzz from last night, and as temporary as it was, she wanted to make it last as long as possible. She turned her dress the right side out and was just placing it over her head when he entered the room.

"I hope you don't need to leave. I just made you breakfast." He was holding a dark wood tray table, with the most wonderful mixture of smells emanating from it, including toast and rich black coffee. She hadn't realised she was hungry until she smelled those delicious aromas.

"No, I don't have to be anywhere." She put her dress down on the armchair and made her way back to the bed, the length of the sheet dragging behind her like a train.

He was wearing a dark navy flannel dressing gown, and his hair was slicked and wet. He looked even more attractive in the light of day. He placed the tray delicately over her legs, and sat beside her, removing the broadsheet newspaper tucked under one arm. There were eggs Benedict, a glass of orange juice, and two cups of black coffee. The cream and sugar cubes sat alongside in antique silverware next to a small matching silver vase with a single yellow rose inside. Marie was extremely impressed. Not only did the food smell wonderful, but the presentation was outstanding. As if he were reading her thoughts, he said, "I like to cook. I find it relaxing. I hope you like the eggs, but if you don't I can easily rustle up something else. Same with the coffee, there's a fresh pot of tea downstairs if you prefer. I should have asked I suppose, but I wanted to surprise you." He smiled that gorgeous smile.

"No, it's wonderful. Thank you. Really, you shouldn't have."

His smile broadened as he reached for one of the cups of coffee and, opening the paper, began to read. As Marie ate, it dawned on her this was not what she expected. When Sara or her girlfriends back home regaled her with tales of one night stands, they had never involved breakfast in bed. In fact, most ended with them being unceremoniously shown the door. Every sitcom or romantic comedy, every story, had indicated that this morning would have involved a walk of shame home with her knickers inside her handbag and a slight headache. But this? This was romance, this was thoughtful consideration, this was.... Marie didn't know what this was. She had prepared herself for an awkward conversation and a quick exit, not courtship.

"Is it alright?"

Marie realised she'd stopped eating and was merely sitting with a bemused look all over her face. "Oh yes, it's delicious. I just, I think I drank a little too much last night. I'm taking it slow."

This appeared to satisfy him, and he went back to reading his paper. Marie watched his hands as he turned the pages. They were incredibly masculine, sensual hands. Hands which last night had touched Marie in ways she never thought possible. She suddenly longed to feel those hands on her skin again. Goosebumps spread over her as the memories of the previous evening swam about her mind.

They sat in silence for a short while, one reading and sipping coffee, the other eating eggs Benedict, but it wasn't an uncomfortable silence. Quite the opposite in fact, Marie felt completely content sitting there beside him. She could have sat there for hours.

After removing the tray, he sat on the bed facing her. "I have a meeting this evening...."

Ah, this is the part where he gets rid of you. She couldn't help feel a tiny bit disappointed. She had known this was coming and had tried to stay above it all, stay emotionless, but she liked him. She couldn't help liking him.

"However, it should only take an hour or so. I would love it, since you said you were available today, if you would go to dinner with me this evening? I could pick you up around eight?"

The instant elation she felt was overwhelming and she struggled to maintain a calm exterior. She didn't want to appear too keen or desperate, especially as he was infuriatingly cool all the time.

"Yes, that would be wonderful."

Chapter Five
-Present Day

It was no use; she would have to give up trying to read. She'd been staring at the same two pages for the best part of fifteen minutes until the words blurred and vanished into the spine. She had too much on her mind to give even an inch of room to Milton. She stared around the library office at the hundreds of books which lined the mahogany shelves, wishing there was some volume among them which would give her all the answers she so desperately needed. This was usually the place she came to forget her worries, but today it wasn't working.

This had been the first room she decorated upon moving in with Malcolm. Most people started with the bedrooms, or lounge, but she had always wanted a room with wall to wall books. There was a large mahogany desk with a green leather top in the centre, a lucky find at an antiques auction, with a green studded club style swivel chair. It was very much modelled on the bar where they had met, with dark wood and brass fixtures. The wall to wall shelving was broken up first by a large marble fireplace, a gold mirror hanging above, and second by a large window which faced into a private garden they shared with the neighbouring houses. This is where Marie placed a large, green leather club chair, to read or sit in quiet contemplation. This is where she sat now with a cream woolen blanket wrapped around her, staring at the trees swaying with the wind.

She thought about the previous evening, the way he had rushed home, the concern in his eyes, and she thought about the phone call she overheard this morning. Something was very wrong with Malcolm, and she could tell he was, for the first time since she'd known him, afraid. She hadn't intended to overhear, she wasn't in the habit of eavesdropping on his conversations. Quite the opposite in fact; she avoided him when he carried out his 'business' calls. She didn't want to know the details of his work, she already knew more than she wanted to know. But that morning, she had been walking past the office on her way to the kitchen and, noticing the door was ajar, found herself slowing, perhaps even tip toeing, as she passed it.

"Did he suffer?"

These words, spoken with obvious pain, made her stop in her tracks. Did who suffer? As far as she was aware, no one they knew had died. There were no funerals to attend or lost loved ones to mourn. But by the way he asked this question, she knew that somewhere, someone Malcolm trusted deeply, and there were few, had died. And they hadn't just died, they had died horribly.

"FUCK." He practically shouted. The pain in his voice replaced with anger, and hatred. "I don't care what the fucking police say, they know what we let them know. I want this handled. I want him dead. I want his family dead. I want every person he's ever fucking smiled at dead."

At the very moment he said 'dead' for the final time the door slammed shut, and the bang echoed throughout the house. She literally jumped with fear, and immediately turned from the door and ran for the downstairs bathroom, locking the door behind her. She was breathing heavily, leaning against the door, her heartbeat pounding loudly in her ears. She was terrified, for so many reasons; she couldn't get her thoughts straight, the words she had just heard reverberating inside her skull like a record with the needle stuck. I want him dead. I want his family dead. I want him dead. So much was wrong with this situation. Malcolm getting emotional for a start; he never got upset; he never showed fear. Something was very wrong. This 'him' was obviously the same man who made Malcolm check on her personally the previous evening, why he had been working late so much lately. He had killed someone important to Malcolm, and Malcolm wanted revenge. Malcolm wanted to murder him, and everyone close to him. And that was the biggest wrong of them all; the fact that this disturbed her less than Malcolm's clearly emotional state. That hearing her husband essentially order a hit on God knows how many people did not disturb her as much as it should. She was upset, yes, frightened even, but she was not surprised. She thought about this for a moment, remembering that night again. The night she arrived home early and found him with that poor man, tied up, helpless. She thought about how she looked into those desperate bloodshot eyes, and turned her back on them.

I want him dead.

After that night, after she made her decision, she accepted what Malcolm was. She chose to stay. But had she considered what that would do to her? Was she as bad as him now? She knew the answer to that question, and it made her feel sick.

She didn't know how long she'd been in the bathroom, but when she emerged she found him drinking scotch in the living room.

"I want you to have a personal body guard, to keep you safe. I've called Mickey, he's on his way now. He will go with you everywhere. Do you understand?" He said all of this without turning around, staring out of the windows. The room was silent apart from the clinking of the ice in his glass every time he took a sip.

"What's happened?"

He turned around and she saw tears were forming on the edge of his lashes, refusing to fall, but refusing to dissipate either. He set the glass down and walked over to her, and placing a hand at either side of her face, he kissed her softly. He looked into her eyes, his hands still cupping her face, and stared at her a moment. She wanted to make it better so badly, she wanted to hold him and make whatever it was go away. But Malcolm wasn't like that. He was a proud man. Whatever this was, he would deal with it alone, he would deal with it his way. "I need you to do this for me, okay?"

"Okay."

The tapping on the door behind her broke her train of thought. It was Mickey. For a moment, curled up in that armchair, she had forgotten he was there in the house, raiding their fridge. "There's someone here to see you, Mrs. Carter."

She looked Mickey up and down. He was a big guy, measuring about six foot five and almost as broad as he was tall. He certainly looked threatening, with his shaved head and the jagged scar on his right cheek, but in reality he was incredibly dim witted; all brawn and no brains. Marie thought he was sweet. He was one of the only employees of Malcolm's that she genuinely liked. She rose from the chair. "Who is it?" She hoped it wasn't her friend Linda or one of the girls from the bar. She wasn't in the mood to socialise, to pretend everything was normal.

"It's a policeman."

She stopped in her tracks. "Did he give a name?"

"He did but I can't remember it, showed me his badge though so he's the real deal. Scottish fellah."

Detective Duncan. What does he want now? "Tell him I'll be right out."

He went to leave, then paused, and looked back at her. "Are you alright Mrs. Carter?"

"I'm fine, why?"

"You've been crying."

She touched her cheek and felt it was damp. She hadn't even realised she was doing it. "I'm fine Mickey, I'm reading a sad book that's all."

He nodded and held out a handkerchief for her. It was embroidered with a football in one corner. She thanked him while wiping her cheeks and eyes, then held it out to him again.

"You keep it, Mrs. Carter, in case the book gets sadder."

She smiled for the first time that day. "Thank you Mickey. Could you tell the detective I'll be out in a moment please?"

"Course, Mrs. Carter."

She closed the door quietly behind him and made her way over to the mirror above the fireplace. She felt like she didn't look quite the same as she had that morning, as if some small, indiscernible change had occurred among the features which made up her face. She could guess why the detective was there. He was there to ask her about a murder, the murder of one of her husband's associates, though she still didn't know who it was. Malcolm hadn't told her anything, and she hadn't asked. He was there to berate her with questions again. She sighed heavily. She didn't know if she had the strength for round two at this very moment in time, but she knew she didn't have a choice.

Chapter Six
-Five Years Ago

When Malcolm's car arrived outside, Marie couldn't have been more relieved. She'd been subjected to a constant barrage of asinine questions from Sara since arriving home that afternoon, and she was becoming more and more irritated. "What does he do? How rich is he? What does his house look like? Was he good in bed?" It was like being interrogated. She hated dissecting the previous evening's events, particularly because she herself still didn't know what it was, or what it could be.

"That's him." She grabbed her bag and carried out a last minute check in the full length mirror before leaving. She'd only brought one fancy outfit with her when she left Northern Ireland, which was the black dress from the evening before. When you only own a suitcase full of belongings, you prioritise the more practical, but jeans and a sweater wouldn't really cut it for a dinner date. Loathe to wear the exact same thing, she had improvised a new outfit, placing the white shirt she used for interviews over the dress, giving the illusion of a skirt and top. It wasn't great, but it would have to do. There was no way she was borrowing any of Sara's items of clothing, despite her insistence. Most of what Sara owned was bright, garish coloured and revealing. Not Marie's style at all. She preferred things to be more simple and classic, and she believed a woman could be sexy without putting everything on display.

After a quick application of her red lipstick and comb of her long black hair, which for this evening she was wearing down and curled, she was ready to go.

"Text me if you're staying at his again. Or should I say when?" Sara laughed at her own joke, and Marie resisted the urge to tell her to mind her own business.

When she got to the front door, she found him standing by his black, chauffeur-driven car, holding a single red rose. He was wearing a dark grey suit and pale blue shirt, this time without a tie, and he looked even more handsome than she remembered. He leaned in to kiss her cheek, softly, and Marie inhaled his aftershave. She felt goose bumps erupt all over her body, and the colour rise to her chest.

"You look stunning."

"Thank you." She accepted the rose, and stepped inside the rear passenger seat as he held open the door for her, before sliding in next to her. Seeing him again caused memories from that night to flash into her mind, appearing suddenly and then vanishing just as quickly. Images of skin and lips and naked flesh. "How was your meeting?"

"It was fine, productive. But I don't want to talk about work. I want to talk about you. I want to get to know you."

"There isn't a lot to tell really."

"Nonsense. Let's start with home, tell me about Ireland."

She started to speak, and paused. She knew this topic of conversation would inevitably come up, but she hadn't thought about how she should respond. She didn't want to dampen the mood; after all, tales of abuse and domestic terrorism were hardly the light hearted 'getting to know you' chit chat of a first date. However, there was something about Malcolm that made her want to be open with him, to be completely honest. Perhaps it was her way of testing him, of pushing to see his true character, in how he would handle such honesty. Or perhaps it was a defense mechanism. If he bolted now, she wouldn't have a chance to fall for him; she wouldn't get hurt. She was torn.

"I sense that's a sensitive topic for you. I understand if you don't want to discuss it, but I really do want to know you better. Warts and all."

For the second time since meeting him, she felt like he could read her mind. It was strangely liberating. "Is that a two-way street?"

"How do you mean?"

"I mean, if I tell you everything about myself, warts and all, will you do the same?"

He thought for a moment, looking at her the entire time, as if he were weighing up invisible odds inside his mind, calculating the risk of complete honesty with her. "How about this. I promise to always be completely honest if you do?"

She was intrigued by this prospect. Exposing oneself so soon could backfire horribly, not just for this fledgling courtship, but for her general self-esteem. However, she had skirted issues, and hidden innermost thoughts with men before and inevitably the relationships had crashed and burned. Surely it made sense to be open from the start, so if one or the other was to be put off, they could bail before it became serious? And, more importantly, she liked him, and she really did want to know him, and for him to know her, completely. Warts and all. Before she could respond, he spoke.

"However, if we do decide on complete honesty from the offset, we should be very careful what questions we ask, as there is always a very strong possibility we won't like the answers we receive."

Marie got the distinct impression that he was talking more about her than about himself, but that only increased her sense of intrigue. What was it about this man, this incredibly attractive and successful man, that she wouldn't like? So far, he seemed so perfect, so charming. But the truth was, no one was perfect, including Marie. She made up her mind; she wanted to know all of him, including his imperfections, and would have to take the risk of exposing her own in order to achieve it. That was a risk she was willing to take. "Alright," she extended her hand to him, which he shook with a crooked smile. "Deal."

Chapter Seven
-Present Day

"Detective Duncan, I was unaware we had anything further to discuss."

He was wearing the same shirt as their first encounter, this time freshly ironed, with a leather jacket over it. He'd also shaved, but it didn't detract from his slightly scruffy image, his longer hairstyle made sure of that. Marie was relieved to see his hands free of any papers or files.

"There have been a few developments, is your husband in?"

He said this in a manner which implied he knew the answer already. Marie was aware the police often monitored her husband's movements, and on more than one occasion she had herself noticed a dark blue car sitting across from the house. "No, but then you already knew that, didn't you?" She didn't try to conceal her irritation; after all, it was warranted. It was bad enough being called to the station on a regular basis, being followed and harassed by police, but now they were making house calls, bringing that oppressive behaviour into her home? She wouldn't allow it.

"Yes I did. I wanted to speak to you alone."

She was a little surprised he admitted to it. The previous detectives had patronised her, and lied to her face on multiple occasions. Honesty was a new approach. "Well, say what you have to say and get out."

They stood a moment, staring at each other awkwardly, and for a split second, Marie thought she glimpsed hurt in his eyes.

"I wanted to apologise, for the other day. I was too heavy handed and I upset you. I'm sorry."

She was completely taken aback. She was prepared for questions, for attitude, not apologies. She had no idea how to respond. They stood in awkward silence for what felt like far too long, each unsure of how to progress. Finally, after reaching saturation point, she had to break it, to say something. "Apology accepted."

He looked visibly relieved, with his shoulders and expression relaxing, which in turn made Marie relax a little as well. The silence became distinctly less awkward, and she found herself warming slightly towards the officer, despite her better judgement.

"What are you reading?"

She looked down at the tatty book in her hand; she had forgotten she was carrying it. "It's Paradise Lost by Milton. It's about the fall of man, the temptation of original sin."

"Ah, well that's something we can all relate to."

"What is?"

"Temptation and sin. We are all guilty."

She eyed him suspiciously. It was clear that there was a hidden meaning behind the comment, but relating to whom she could not decide. Her husband, perhaps, or maybe herself. Or perhaps the detective was referring to himself. She was intrigued. "Surely, as a police officer, a symbol for justice and good, surely that wouldn't include yourself?" She didn't try to hide the sarcasm. She had personally witnessed the hypocrisy of the police failing to practice what they preached. She knew for a fact that several were employed by her husband, having seen the bribes being passed inside newspapers and bags. It surprised her initially, but after meeting so many, so regularly, she'd gradually seen them as what they truly were – weak. A dog with no teeth. He didn't seem phased however, quite the opposite in fact, as he smiled at her wryly. He reminded her of a little boy who had just been caught with his hand in the biscuit tin.

He stepped towards her, now only a couple of feet away. "I'm just as flawed and weak as any other man. Just as easily tempted by an easy fix, or a pretty face." He emphasised the last, slowing down his speech as he said it, staring her square in the eye. Marie felt her heart beat increase, and she swallowed hard. He was an attractive man, making it clear he found her attractive, and this situation had become extremely unfamiliar to her. Since she began dating Malcolm all those years ago, no man would have dared to come on to her, knowing it might incur his wrath. Malcolm was not known as a forgiving man. She had forgotten what it felt like, to be desired by someone new. But, the question was why? Why was this man, this officer, attempting to flirt with her? Was it a ploy perhaps, to put her off guard or get her onside? She couldn't help but be suspicious.

He broke the silence first. "The difference between me and the men I arrest is, I try to do what's right. I strive to be a good man."

This time the meaning was more obvious, and it was clear to Marie he was talking about her husband. This got her back up a little, but only slightly, because deep down, she knew he was right. Her husband had made a choice, just like she had, and once you begin down that path, there's no way back. "It's easy to judge another man when you haven't walked a day in his shoes."

She mulled these words over, repeating them in her mind. When you haven't walked a day in his shoes. She had always considered her path through life a fairly difficult one, but it was nothing when compared to Malcolm's. When she heard his life story, she'd felt ashamed of the chip she carried around on her shoulder all those years. No matter how hard your journey has been, there is always another whose woes were far worse. And Malcolm was a man who had had a hard walk in life, in the beginning anyway.

She recalled the evening of their first date, when they made a promise to one another. A promise to be honest, to share their collective histories, unedited. She spoke about Northern Ireland. About how her father had been a failed paramilitary. He was the type of man who considered himself to be hard, but was, in reality, weak. He'd signed up to the Ulster Volunteer Force at eighteen and carried out their dirty work for years, convincing himself he was 'one of the boys' when he was merely a lackey. A fact he discovered, much to his dismay, when he was caught by the RUC beating the hell out of a Catholic stranger;

an act carried out at the order of his compatriots. They completely abandoned him at that point, leaving him to the mercy of the judge, and as a result his world was crushed and his identity stripped from him. He turned to alcohol, and made himself feel 'manly' again by beating his wife, Marie's mother, and on one occasion Marie herself. Her mother had given up long before Marie entered the world and her siblings had scattered, a brother following a similar fate as the father and a sister who was pregnant at thirteen with a man not dissimilar from their father. They'd lived in a run-down council house in South Belfast, amongst abandoned white goods and sectarian graffiti. Marie's grandmother had been her only light in life, and when she died, she became determined to escape, to start fresh. Of course, it was different now. As she had grown she saw the violence lessen, and the regeneration of the city. She'd seen the forming of the PSNI and the handshakes and talks between old enemies, now colleagues. But that determination had never left, and the minute she could afford to leave, she had. Yes, she thought her upbringing was sad, but it was nothing when compared to Malcolm's.

There were similarities. Malcolm too had grown up in a poor council estate, and he too had a violent father with criminal links, but this was where their stories differed. Malcolm's father had been a well-respected member of a prominent criminal organisation. He carried out murders and beatings at the order of the boss, a man named Mark Henry. Although he was clearly capable of violence, this was never directed at Malcolm or his mother, whom he loved dearly. He raised Malcolm to be strong, to know how to look after himself, which was essential in the area in which they lived. He taught him how to shoot, got him into boxing so he knew how to fight, but more importantly he pushed Malcolm to go to school, to study, something he had always regretted not doing. He wanted his son to succeed where he had failed, to get out of that place and be somebody, but truthfully Malcolm wanted to be like his father. He worshipped him, and at thirteen, when he was forced to watch as four men beat him to death, his world ended. His father had refused to carry out an order, to kill a local snitch, a traitor to the organisation, along with his wife and his two small children. He was a killer, but not a child killer. This was deemed to be disloyalty, verging on mutiny for Mark Henry, and was met with swift and brutal punishment. Malcolm's mother, who had also been forced to watch, fled with him to stay with family just outside the city. She tried to carry on where her husband left off, raising Malcolm, educating him, but she never recovered from the events of that evening and no one was particularly surprised when she took the overdose. Malcolm found her. At fifteen, he was orphaned and bitter, but he stayed the course, attending school and eventually university, because that's what his father would have wanted. He'd made a success of his life.

All of this was the truth, and sharing it brought them closer. But Malcolm had not been ready to tell the rest of the story that evening, choosing to end it there, in order to protect her. It wasn't until much later, when Marie asked directly, that she discovered what kind of a success Malcolm really was. Only then did he tell her the rest of his tale. About how, in the back of his mind, he had always harboured a plan for revenge. How at the age of twenty-seven, after several years of planning, infiltrating the organisation his father had worked for, moving up the ranks, he earned their trust. Waiting patiently until he was Mark Henry's right hand man, before putting a bullet between his eyes. Of how he had taken over. He succeeded alright, he got the revenge he craved and he was now powerful and rich, but at what cost? Marie thought hard about that the day she made her decision to stay. She asked that question so many times, asked herself whether or not he had become the very man he had despised. Whether or not he was the new Mark Henry.

"Mrs. Carter? Marie?"

She jolted back to the present day. The detective was looking at her with concern; clearly her mind had gotten away from her. She wondered how long she'd been lost in thought. Long enough, clearly. "I appreciate the apology, but if that's all, then I am going to have to ask you to leave."

He stared at her for a few seconds, that same look he'd given her at the station. That look seemed to be ever present when he was around her. "Of course." He turned towards the door, opening it slowly, and after taking an initial step forwards, he paused, still facing outside, his back to her. Marie, who had been following him out, came to an abrupt stop behind him. "Look, I know you don't want to talk to me. I know you won't and I get it, I understand your feelings of loyalty. I do. But there are things at work here which you have no idea about, things that you need to know." He turned to face her. "Please, if you ever need help, or just someone to speak to, for anything, please call me. Please."

The look in his eyes made Marie shudder. This time it wasn't just concern, there was fear there, but about what she could not determine. Fear for her, fear for himself, she wasn't sure. But what she did know was that she had seen that exact look before. She had seen it on Malcolm when he rushed home to her.

"What are you talking about?"

"I can't, I've already said too much. There are rules, data protection, I can't. Ask your husband, just ask him." He went to leave again, this time in more of a hurry, but once just outside the doorway he paused again, just long enough to utter one sentence. "Ask him about Jonathan Savage."

Chapter Eight
-Five Years Ago

Marie was on cloud nine when she arrived home that day. It was the morning after their eighth date and she felt euphoric. They'd spent the past two weeks dancing and eating and kissing. But mostly, they talked. They talked and talked about everything and anything. Their childhoods, their fears, their favourite films, their mutual hopes to one day have a family. She shared things with him she had never told anyone except her grandmother. Sometimes, on their dates, she felt like they were the only two people on earth. And it felt wonderful.

"So you're still alive then? I was about to send out a search party." It was Sara, emerging from her bedroom. Based on the strong smell of alcohol and her streaked make-up, it was clear she hadn't been overly concerned.

"I texted you, you knew where I was."

"Well you missed the most amazing party last night." There was a moan from inside Sara's room. Clearly. "Oh God he's waking up. I have to fix myself before he sees me in the daylight."

And with that she was off to the bathroom, leaving Marie to her thoughts. She went into the kitchen, and after making herself a cup of tea, she sat down at the laptop they shared. Between work and Malcolm, she hadn't had time to check her emails or Facebook and she was feeling rather cut off from the world. But the truth was, she was OK with that. She had never been into social media, and used it purely as a means of staying in contact with old friends back home. What she was really doing was procrastinating, trying to avoid a thought that just kept popping up inside her mind, no matter how hard she tried to ignore it. You're falling in love with him. She tried to shake it off. It was a ridiculous thing to think, to feel. This man had been a complete stranger only a couple of weeks ago. She was a fool if she thought she truly knew him well enough to feel that level of emotion. Maybe you don't need to.

No. Love wasn't like it was portrayed in films. Marie had never believed in love at first sight. She thought it was something that would take time. Yet, every moment she was with him she had a feeling that only a word of that magnitude could describe, and it frightened her. She'd been in relationships before, but she never loved any of them. One of her boyfriends had told her he loved her once, and she ended it then and there because she knew she would never feel the same, and she thought that was the kindest thing to do.

She was afraid to be in love, because she didn't know how to be. The only long term relationships she'd been around were filled with resentment and sadness. Her parents. Her sister. Love hadn't worked out well for them. That's why she always protected herself, by trying to see men and relationships as temporary relief, not as long term commitments. But now, all she wanted to do was spend every waking moment with Malcolm. Would the 'L' world ruin that too? And worse, what if she did face her fears and let herself plunge head first and he didn't feel the same? What if he didn't love her back?

Marie felt sick. It had been two days of these thoughts, going round and round in circles inside her head until she felt nauseous. It was during moments like this she wished, more than ever, that her grandmother was still alive. She would do anything to ask her advice now, to hear her share the story for the millionth time of how she had ended up with Marie's grandfather.

They were childhood friends and neighbours. Her grandfather Hugh told her grandmother Annie, at the tender age of five, that he loved her and wanted to marry her. She had laughed in his face. He would have to wait fifteen years to hear her say the words back. They remained inseparable for their entire lives, sharing every experience and heartache together, but not once while growing up had she looked at him as anything other than her goofy mate. It took an explosion to make her see otherwise. It was the height of the troubles, and at twenty years old, Annie was a nurse at the Royal Victoria Hospital, Hugh a factory worker. She was on duty when news of the bomb came in. It was nothing unusual, sadly. She hated the fighting, they both did, and refused to take sides, hoping any day would bring peace. But this bomb had been planted at the factory, and reports stated that the building collapsed with everyone inside. She felt physically sick. Marie's grandmother had always been a stoic woman, brave and capable in the face of anything; that's what made her such a good nurse. But at this news, she simply crumbled. Why hadn't she realised before, just how important he was to her? Why had she never told him how much she needed him, how much she cared? She had been a fool, and now it was too late. She collapsed under the weight of these sudden realisations and ended up on one of the hospital's beds herself, being tended to by her colleagues. They had no idea what was wrong with her, she wouldn't speak, and were genuinely concerned for her welfare, so they were relieved when her friend Hugh came to see why she hadn't returned home from her shift that day. Her grandmother described how she awoke to find him praying over her, begging God to help her pull through whatever the affliction was. She thought she was dreaming at first, but when he opened his eyes and saw her, when he kissed her, she knew it was real and she felt happiness and relief wash over her. It turned out her grandfather had chosen to skive off work for the day in order to get drunk at the local bar. Her grandmother always laughed at that part of the story. When Marie thought of love, that's what she thought of.

Could this really compare? Two weeks of dinner dates and amazing sex is hardly a steady foundation on which to build a relationship. She was so confused. She took a sip of her tea and realised it was stone cold. She must have been sitting like that for an age. She re-boiled the kettle, and after hearing the front door open and shut after a few murmurs, she took another cup down from the cupboard. Sara entered a moment later with a huge grin on her now clean face. "Tea?"

"Coffee, black. I have the hangover from Hell."

"Well you don't look very hungover. In fact, you look more like the cat that got the cream."

Sara laughed as Marie set the mug of steaming coffee in front of her. "He is pretty great."

"Did you meet him last night?"

"No. That's the third time I've seen him this week. I met him about a year ago. We would see each other from time to time, but recently it got more serious."

Marie was surprised. Sara rarely saw a man more than once, twice at a push. This one was obviously different. "Do you like him?"

"Actually, I love him. And he loves me too. He told me last night." Sara's face lit up as she said it, her smile wide, and Marie was desperately trying to hide the look of sheer shock on her face. Sara always said love was a fiction created by people to give their lives more meaning. She had always been cynical about it, more so than Marie, and to hear her use the word so freely now was more than a little strange. She proceeded to regale Marie with the tale of how they met at a bar, how a one-night stand quickly became a friendship with benefits, and now a full blown relationship. His name was Charlie, and he was a DJ and musician at several local bars. He was poor, and the fact that this didn't bother Sara was shocking. That was always her plan; to meet and marry some rich man and live comfortably. Obviously her priorities changed. She gushed about how he was different than other men, about how he made her feel special. It was obvious to Marie that Sara was happier than she'd seen her in years. And she was happy for her, for them, but she was also a little jealous of Sara's clarity, of her assuredness. Here she was wrestling with what she thought she was feeling, and Sara had just gone for it. She admired her bravery.

"You want to see him?" She typed into the still open laptop and brought up his Facebook profile. He was a handsome guy, with dark brown eyes and long dirty, fair hair. He had several tattoos and piercings which added to his 'rocker' look.

Marie could see the appeal. "He's cute."

"Damn right he is. We could all get a drink this weekend, me and my man, and you and yours? Introductions are necessary."

"Maybe it's a little early for that."

Sara shrugged. "Suit yourself, but I have to meet him eventually. Get him up on Facebook now so I can at least see what he looks like."

"He doesn't have a Facebook page. He doesn't use sites like that."

"That's weird, who doesn't have some kind of internet profile these days?"

"He's not really into that kind of thing."

"I maintain that it's weird. Are you sure though? Maybe he said he doesn't because he's married and didn't want you seeing the pictures of his adoring children? Did you at least google him?"

Marie laughed, "I'm not going to internet stalk him. I trust him."

"Alright, suit yourself. I'm gonna take a shower." She got up, taking the remainder of her coffee with her, and made her way for the door.

Marie's mind was still so muddled, her feelings so unclear, and she was desperate to ask Sara one question. "How do you know?"

Sara stopped and turned to face her. "How do I know what?"

"How do you know you love him?"

That big wide smile stretched across the length of Sara's face once more. "When you know, you know."

Chapter Nine
-Present Day

As soon as the Detective left, she made her way back to the office, to the laptop computer sitting on the mahogany desk. Jonathan Savage. Jonathan Savage. Over and over again she repeated it in her mind, determined she wouldn't forget it. But how could she? Everything that happened that day, the exchange with Detective Duncan, it had unnerved her in more ways than one. That name would forever be associated with the strange conversation, with the look on his face; the look on her husband's face. There are things at work here which you have no idea about, things that you need to know. What did he mean? What was going on? She hated this feeling, the feeling that you're the only person in a room who has no idea what's going on.

As soon as the computer was on, she opened google and typed the name, her fingers hitting each key with unnecessary force.

"J-O-N-A-T-H-A-N S-A-V-A-G-E." But then she stopped, her finger hovering just millimeters above the Enter key. Is this the right thing to do? Her mind was racing, a jumbled chaotic mass of questions and emotions. If she did hit enter, what would she find?

Would it even be the truth? She had learned over the years that journalists had a habit of sensationalising events, or completely overlooking facts, in search of what would sell the most copies. Her husband had the best barristers in the country, and any hint of mistruth or libelous information about her husband or herself, was met with swift and efficient legal action. Most journalists had learned to avoid even mentioning the name Malcolm Carter. It had become too expensive to do so. She would never be able to decipher the truth from fiction; surely it would raise more questions than it answered? She would only receive odd pieces of a larger jigsaw puzzle, but never enough to form the actual picture. It might simply make things worse.

Then, there was the niggling feeling that she was going behind Malcolm's back. That by seeking the information out and choosing not to simply ask him, she was somehow betraying him. That she was saying she didn't trust him to know what was best. Surely if something was truly wrong, he would have told her? But something was very wrong, she knew that. But, the main reason she stepped away from the computer was because of one question. A question glaring at her from the screen. Do I really want to know?

When she came home early that fateful evening, all those years ago, when she had seen what Malcolm really did, laid out in front of her in all its bloody glory, she decided to stay, yes, but she made it perfectly clear that she wanted nothing to do with that part of his life. She loved him too much to go, and she still did, so she simply ignored that part of his life. She would never ask about his work, or read another newspaper again. As far as she was concerned, it wasn't any of her business. She hadn't come to that decision lightly of course, and she still wrestled with her guilt, but that was the decision she made and she couldn't go back and change it now. It was far too late for that. For a second, she saw that man's eyes, pleading with her, begging her for help. The man she left to die.

If she asked Malcolm about Jonathan Savage, the barrier of ignorance she spent four years so carefully building would come crashing down around her. And she was afraid. She was afraid that this time she might not be able to simply turn her back and close her eyes. Afraid that the reality of the situation, the reality of his work, of who he is outside of them, would be too much for her to simply ignore anymore. She knew once she started asking questions, once she began down that path, there was no turning back, and that terrified her.

By the time she heard Malcolm's voice in the corridor, she'd been in that office, pacing back and forth for almost two hours, and she was exhausted, both physically and emotionally.

"Sweetheart, are you alright? Mickey said some police officer came over and upset you. I'll have his badge."

He put his arms around her, and she sank her head into his chest and inhaled deeply. She always felt so safe in his arms, like nothing could hurt her as long as she was by his side. She longed to stay like that indefinitely, but she knew what she had to do, what she was always going to have to do at some point. "Tell me about Jonathan Savage."

Chapter Ten
-Five Years Ago

The day Marie knew for certain she was in love with Malcolm wasn't a particularly special one. Nothing out of the ordinary had happened, nor was it an especially romantic moment. After a few months of regular dinner dates, and sleepovers at Malcolm's loft, she knew she was infatuated, yes, but the idea of love still felt premature. They had spent the evening at an art exhibition opening in a gallery Malcolm owned. It was described in the programme as 'A Modernist, dystopic view of a world consumed by shallow Capitalism', but Marie had struggled to see this message in the small, solitary red and black squares painted on the mammoth sized canvases. They drank champagne together, whilst laughing about how pretentious the entire thing was. Malcolm preferred more classic art, and Marie preferred something that involved more skill than tracing a square. It had been, like all of their dates, a perfect evening.

When she awoke the next morning to the smell of pancakes, she dressed in Malcolm's pale blue shirt and made her way towards the delicious smells emanating from the open plan kitchen. It occurred to her that if life were like the cartoons she had watched as a child, she would currently be floating amongst the drawn wisps of that scent. The idea made her giggle to herself. Malcolm was standing at the large range cooker, with his back to her, flipping the pancakes like a pro. She stood a moment watching him, admiring both his culinary skills and his muscular toned back.

"It's rude to stare, you know."

He hadn't even turned around. How did he know I was there? On more than one occasion she'd had the impression that Malcolm had some kind of sixth sense. Not only did he always seem to read her like a book, but he was impossible to sneak up on. "I wasn't staring, I was ogling. That's an entirely different thing."

"Ah, well in that case, ogle away."

He smiled that smile which made her go distinctly weak at the knees, and feeling like a foolish giddy school girl, she hurried to the large, reclaimed table. A moment later, he brought over the plates, one for each of them, and sat opposite her. The pancakes had suspicious purple spots amongst the fluffy batter, and she feared the worst.

"Are those blueberry?" Marie hated the idea of Malcolm's clear efforts having gone to waste, and of turning her nose up at the breakfast he'd been kind enough to prepare for her. But the fact was, she hated blueberries more.

"No, no of course not. I know you hate blueberries. They're blackberries. I remember you saying how much you loved them because they reminded you of going fruit picking with your grandmother."

"Aw thank you! They're perfect." She smiled,

and was about to pour over the maple syrup when the idea suddenly struck her, like lightening, I love him. She knew this suddenly, and with complete certainty, as if she had all of a sudden remembered the answer to a question no one had asked. The pancakes, so thoughtful and sweet, the fact that he listened to her so intently and remembered such a trivial fragment of their conversations together, it all made her so happy. He made her so happy, and she loved him, she knew that now. She was still trying to process this information when his voice interrupted her train of thought.

"Are they okay? If you don't like them, I could make you something else?"

She realised she had just been sitting staring at her plate, and she blushed, embarrassed by how easily her emotions paralysed her. She mumbled they were fine, and ate with double the enthusiasm necessary.

I love him. These three words were echoing around inside her head, and the noise they were making was not diminishing. They were just three words, which separately were so non-threatening, so innocuous, but when combined in that order they implied so much. She was feeling so many emotions at once. Happiness was definitely amongst them. He made her happy, they made each other happy, and to love someone was a joyous thing. But the happiness was overshadowed by overwhelming fear. She was afraid. Afraid that things were moving too quickly, afraid that she was going to ruin what they had by making it into something serious or by labelling it in a particular way. After all, they hadn't even discussed what this was between them. But most of all, she realised her greatest fear was the fear of rejection. Quite simply, what if he didn't feel the same way? What if she told him, and he couldn't return the sentiment by uttering the words in return? It would be humiliating, and it would irreparably damage what they had together. The whole thing made her head hurt.

He seemed to sense something was wrong, because he had stopped eating his pancakes and his paper was now neatly folded beside him. "What are you thinking?"

Oh God, what a question to have asked! Any question but that one. She considered lying, a few options for a tall tale entering her mind. I'm fine, I'm just not feeling well or I'm just tired. Either would work just as well as the other, but the believability of her fib or the gullibility of Malcolm were not what stopped her from uttering the words. It was the promise she had made to him, a promise to be honest, always. There was nothing for it, she would have to tell him the truth, but she would never be brave enough to mention the 'L' word, not first anyway. Instead she went for something vague, in an attempt to skirt along the edge of truth, telling herself omission doesn't necessarily constitute a lie. She was unaware until later that Malcolm had used the same logic when he discussed his work. She swallowed hard. "I was thinking about us; about what this is."

She hated herself for saying it. It sounded like a line from an American sitcom, but it was true and it was miles better than saying something like I was thinking about how I have fallen completely in love with you. She was afraid to make eye contact with him, so she stared at her half eaten pancakes hard enough for the purple of the blackberries and the beige of the batter to blur and swirl together.

"Ah, I see. I suppose this conversation had to happen eventually."

Her heart began to pound hard inside her chest until she could feel the pulse in her neck, convinced the sentence she just uttered spelled the beginning of the end for their relationship, or whatever this would be called. He would be too gentlemanly to unceremoniously dump her right now right here, he would ease her down gently, giving her the option to accept things as they were or move on elsewhere. She was angry with herself for being so needy.

"I'm not seeing anyone other than you, in fact I haven't been interested in any other women since the night we met. I consider you, and refer to you to others, as my girlfriend. I consider this a relationship. Is that what you meant?"

Is it what I meant? It was and it wasn't. She was elated to hear him refer to her as his girlfriend. He was validating their relationship, and acknowledging that it was serious for him. It was a huge relief, that was true, but she couldn't help feeling a little disappointed that he hadn't mentioned love at any point. She felt foolish for being disappointed for not receiving something she hadn't even expected. He moved towards her, and placed his hand gently on the side of her face, tilting it so she had no choice but to look him square in the eye. "I'm in love with you. I think I've loved you from the first moment I saw you."

Her heart seemed to stop. The pulse in her neck stopped. The world around her stopped. In that moment, she felt as if she had never been and could never again be this happy. She felt like they were the only people on earth, and as she kissed him, she wished she could stay in that perfect moment forever. "I love you too."

Chapter Eleven
-Present Day

She stared out of the window at the murky darkness of London permeated by thousands of dots of light. A childhood memory drifted into her mind, of hiding inside a blanket 'fort', light piercing the shadowed interior through the moth eaten fabric, trying not to hear the noise of her parents shouting outside, before fading just as quickly. The city outside so busy, so full of life, seemed in stark contrast to the deathly silence inside their home. It seemed to Marie, like a muffled silence, as if the house itself was holding its breath waiting for her response.

She adjusted the focus of her eyes, turning her attention to the scene inside the study, and to Malcolm himself. He was on his haunches by a dying fire, occasionally and absentmindedly nudging at it with a wrought iron poker. It would send a scattering of embers into the draft of the chimney, like fire bugs escaping to the cold streets outside. His face was drawn and for the first time she noticed lines etched around his forehead, as if each concern had left a permanent scar on his handsome face. He appeared to be sapped of energy, the worries and stress he'd been hiding from her for so many months, the battles he'd fought, lost and won, had clearly taken their toll on him. He looked tired.

Part of her wanted to go to him, to hold him, to comfort him as much as herself, but she couldn't. Her anger, her fears, whilst beginning to subside and die with the fire, were ever present and still very much felt. How could he not have told me? How could he keep this from me? She was unsure how long they'd been in that room, it felt like hours, and neither had spoken for a long time. All of what had been said that night swam inside her head, creating a feeling of pressure, as if the thoughts themselves were trying to force their way out.

What she knew now was this: Jonathan Savage was born and raised in the notorious Aylesbury Estate in South London. His father was a thug, who didn't so much raise his son as beat him into adulthood, and his mother was a heroin addict and prostitute who died with a needle in her arm when Jonathan was just three years old. The alarm was raised when neighbours found Jonathan wandering naked through the estate. His father was drunk at a nearby pub and declined to return in a hurry when he was notified, choosing instead to finish his pint. As most of the disenfranchised youth did in areas like this, he joined a gang at an early age, and quickly proved himself worthy one armed robbery and stabbing at a time. The years of abuse he suffered at the hand of his father had twisted and broken him, turning him into a cruel and cold man, incapable of empathy. By the age of twenty, he had killed three men, including a police officer, elevating him to a level of infamy which demanded a certain amount of respect amongst his peers.

But Jonathan didn't care about old fashioned things like respect. What he valued was unbridled fear. He wanted people to quake at the mere mention of his name, and so at only twenty-four years old, Jonathan and a band of loyal and sadistic followers massacred their way across the estate, and beyond, torturing and murdering every rival drug dealer, gang member and independent criminal. Those who were left alive were spared in exchange for their declaration of loyalty to Jonathan and the new gang he created out of blood and bone.

Jonathan had since built an empire. As well as drugs, he was involved in human trafficking (often involving girls as young as ten), prostitution, arms dealing, robbery, and murder for cash. He also allegedly enjoyed raping, beating and occasionally killing young women, but as those he targeted were either too afraid to report the matter to police or were one of the poor Eastern European women he had trafficked and gotten hooked on his cheap, tainted heroin, this merely remained a persistent rumour.

Police, despite their best efforts, had been unable to get him for anything – an alibi was never in short supply for Jonathan Savage. He was a sadist, who enjoyed inflicting pain and who, more often than out of necessity, killed for the sheer pleasure he took in it. It was in this fact that Jonathan and Malcolm were polar opposites.

Malcolm had murdered people, yes, both with his own hands, and by extension, through his goons acting on his orders, but at no point had he done so out of pleasure. The one and only time that a killing had come even close was when he murdered Mark Henry. But that had been out of loyalty to his father, out of a sense of honour and duty, and any pleasure taken from it was born out of the relief of having finally completed a task fourteen years in the making, rather than in the act itself. The men Malcolm killed were assassins sent from rival criminals. They were members of his own organisation who were leaking information to the police or to his rivals. In Malcolm's underworld, their deaths were considered necessary, for the survival of his empire, for his survival and for mine. Jonathan however, killed because he could and because he enjoyed it, and he did so regularly and with vigour. That made him the type of person who, even to a man like Malcolm, appeared to be some kind of monster.

Jonathan was a new generation of criminal. Malcolm came from an age of mutual understanding and respect amongst the criminal underworld. Jonathan, his attitude, and his methods, spat in the face of everything Malcolm believed and had worked so hard to establish. At first, Malcolm heard bits and pieces of information from his men, nothing which overly concerned him at the time. Perhaps this was out of arrogance, or a sense of invincibility after the many years he had sat atop the throne, and the many potential usurpers he'd seen perish at his hand. But soon, reports came of attacks on his men, of shipments he arranged being hijacked, and of several of his business premises being burned out. Jonathan had declared war on Malcolm.

With every attack, Malcolm hit back with an

equal blow against his opponent, and so it continued for the past two months. A bloody battle was raging on the streets of London between the old generation and the new, and there had been losses on each side. But gradually, the tides began to turn in favour of Jonathan, and Malcolm, for the first time in many, many years, was losing.

And so, it was in the midst of this madness that Malcolm had come face to face with his own mortality. Yesterday, while leaving Capone's after a particularly fruitful business meeting with an 'overseas investor', Malcolm realised he left his watch inside the bar's office. The watch had belonged to his grandfather, then his father, and now him. A gold vintage Rolex, it was the only thing of value his father ever owned, and even in the toughest of times, had refused to sell. He wore it always, for luck, removing it only to wash his hands or, as on this occasion, change his shirt. He sent his driver on, asking him to heat the interior of the car, he would only be a moment.

The explosion was deafening, engulfing the car in flames in an instant and incinerating the driver inside, turning him to blackness and smoke. It had torn through the street, shattering every nearby window, and severely injuring pedestrians and drivers nearby, placing one in intensive care. It was clear who the bomb had been meant for, and how close Malcolm had come to death, and for the first time since the battle lines had been drawn, he thought about what would happen to Marie if he was killed, what Jonathan would do to her, what he could do to her. He felt her loss, almost as if it was she burning inside that car, and it terrified him to his core. The idea of losing her, of her being hurt because of him, was devastating. She thought about his return that night, the missed calls, the look on his face, the way he'd held her.

But that wasn't the end of this bloody tale, Marie knew that much. The phone conversation she overheard that morning had been replayed so many time inside her head, she could transcribe it. I want him dead. I want his family dead. "What happened this morning?"

At first, he made no motion to move from his spot by the dying embers of the fire, the dull glow casting shadows on his features, emphasising his facial expressions all the more. Eventually, after what felt like a long time, he stood and turned to face her. "Richard's dead."

That was all he said. Those two words, whispered rather than spoken, were wrought with so much sadness, Marie thought for a moment that Malcolm was going to cry, something she had never seen.

But the sadness passed quickly along his face like a wave and gave way to anger, and hatred. And Marie understood why; Richard had been his friend and ally since he had begun his journey all those years ago. He'd been there when he first returned to London, he'd been there when Mark Henry had fallen, and he'd been there when Malcolm took power. Apart from Marie, Richard had been the only human alive whom Malcolm truly trusted.

"How?"

"He was taken sometime during the night. He was tortured and dismembered. His body, or most of it, was found this morning by bin men."

Marie had met Richard a hundred times over the years. He was a serious, quiet man, who spoke very little but said a lot with a simple expression or gesture. She had witnessed so many silent conversations between he and Malcolm; moments where Richard would simply look at him over his sunglasses, his grey eyes only a shade darker than his grey hair, conveying all the information in that split second, before Malcolm would simply nod. Despite all the years, and the fact that Richard had always been there, a constant presence in her new life, Marie now realised she knew very little about him, and that thought suddenly made her very sad.

Her memories wandered to his wife, Linda, and their two-year-old son, Elijah, and suddenly a thought struck her hard, a terrible, black thought, too horrible to fathom. Where are they? With Richard killed the way he was, they would have immediately come here to the house. Malcolm would be protecting them, taking care of them. That's what Richard would have wanted, what he would have done for her, should something have happened to Malcolm.

She stared hard at Malcolm, the words rising like bile in her mouth, "Where are Linda and Elijah?" He didn't have to answer her, his pained, twisted expression telling her everything she dreaded most in that moment. They were dead, both of them.

A wave of nausea flooded over her, and she began to shake. Through the blur of tears she saw him reach toward her hand and she pulled it back instinctively. She wasn't ready to end this conversation, not yet. She needed to know what happened, she needed to know everything, because only then could it become real to her. She swallowed hard, trying to keep the tears back, trying to keep the nausea down. Her lips were so dry all of a sudden, and the only sound she could hear was her own jagged breathing. "What happened?" She said it so quietly, a whimper more than words.

"I don't think...."

"TELL ME!" She screamed the words at him, the overwhelming sadness being momentarily overridden by anger. He would not decide what was best for her, not this time.

Minutes passed, until the shock on Malcolm's face slowly subsided, giving way to resignation. He looked away, back at the ever darkening fireplace, unable to hold her gaze. "Elijah's throat was slit while he slept. I don't think he suffered," he trailed off for a moment, like the words were simply too painful to say out loud, "Linda was.... she was.... they raped her before they stabbed her to death. I'm sorry. I'm so so sorry."

Everything around her started swimming, the room, Malcolm, the furniture, it started to blur and twist around, swirling together alongside her memories of Richard's spaghetti carbonara, of the scent of Linda's perfume, of Elijah's chubby little smile, until all she could see as she lost consciousness was the fireplace, now dark and cold. Dead like her friends.

Chapter Twelve
-Five Years Ago

When she opened the door, she expected to find Malcolm there, but instead she found the huge frame of a rather intimidating looking man looming over her. He announced he was her driver and was to take her to a secret location to meet Malcolm. His broad smile revealed a couple of missing teeth, as well as one very shiny, gold one, and he seemed uncomfortable in the suit he wore, shifting his weight back and forth and constantly adjusting his tie. His sheer mass made him seem like someone she should be very afraid of, and Marie had no doubt she should probably never get on his bad side, but he spoke so kindly to her that she instantly took to him.

"What should I wear?"

"I'm sure whatever you wear will be perfect Miss."

"Well I don't know what we're doing when we get there. Is what I'm wearing now okay?"

He looked her up and down a couple of times, studying the hounds tooth dress. "I think you look beautiful Miss. Truly."

She smiled at him, and he suddenly blushed, tugging at the knot of his grey tie. The thing looked like it was straining under the width of his neck.

"Why don't you take that off? It looks uncomfortable."

"Mr. Carter wanted me to look smart. He told me, he said, "Mickey dress smart" and this is my best suit. I wear it for funerals and weddings."

"I think you'd look just as smart without the tie."

He seemed to ponder this for a moment, his hand resting on the tie, pressing it against his broad chest. "Really?"

"Really."

He didn't seem to require any further reassurance, and within a second the tie was undone and in his jacket pocket. His relief was obvious and instantaneous.

"There, just as smart, Mr.....?"

"Mickey, Miss. Just Mickey."

The car took a familiar route, and stopped outside Capone's. Marie was a little disappointed. The driver picking her up, telling her he was taking her to a 'secret location', Malcolm making Mickey wear his Sunday best. She had expected something dramatic, or at least unfamiliar. They'd spent nights here dozens of times over the course of their relationship. Quite frankly, it was a little anti-climactic.

When she entered the club, she was surprised to find it completely empty. Normally on a Friday night it was heaving, but as she walked along, her footsteps echoed in the silence. When she came to the stairs she saw Malcolm sitting at their usual booth, an ice bucket and two glasses of champagne on the table. He stood to greet her, and as they embraced, the stage lights suddenly illuminated to reveal a band. Marie, momentarily startled, took a moment to recognise the singer as the one she'd heard on her first night in the bar all those months ago. The drummer counted them in, and she began to sing It Had To Be You in her warm, caramel tone.

"Will you dance with me?

"Of course."

They didn't move onto the dance floor, there was no need since there were no other people to jostle. He held her tightly against him as they swayed back and forth, the familiar smell of him engulfing her. "Do you recognise the song?"

She raised her head from his chest. "Of course, everyone knows this song."

"Yes, but it's not that. It was the song that was playing the first moment I saw you."

She felt a small pang of guilt. She couldn't remember the music from that night. "I hadn't realised, sorry."

"No, no don't be sorry. I just wanted to show you how much that night means to me, how much you mean to me."

"I know; I feel the same way."

He stopped moving, but continued to hold her there, his hand resting in the small of her back. "Marie, my life, it can be so complicated. My work is difficult sometimes, and after all these years I had given up on the idea of finding someone, but then you came along and surprised me. And with you, it's all so simple. You make everything better, you make me so happy. I love you."

"I love you too."

"Well then, marry me."

"What?"

"I'm asking you to marry me." He released her hand and reached inside his jacket pocket to reveal a small, red velvet box, the other hand still squeezing her against him. "I had thought about a big elaborate display of love, but it all seemed so hollow. I thought where better to ask you than here, where we first met, where my life changed forever for the better. Marry me."

She was speechless, overwhelmed with emotion. She felt so much happiness and love in that moment, she felt like she could explode. The words she spoke were barely audible, a squeak rather than a shout, just about making it out as the tears fell down her cheeks. "Yes....yes."

Only then did he release her, opening the box to reveal an antique, Art Deco ring. A large diamond sat surrounded by sparkling sapphires, her birth stone. It was stunning, and it fit perfectly. It felt right. They danced for hours, they drank champagne, and for that night she felt as if they were the only two people on earth.

"I would do anything for you Marie. I would die for you." He pulled her closer to him, squeezing her gently. "I would kill for you."

Chapter Thirteen
-Present Day

It started with a cup of coffee.

After that night in the study, after the revelations and tears, everything about her life which had once seemed so solid, so certain, suddenly felt so precarious that even the smallest, slightest breeze would bring everything crashing down. She hadn't felt this unsure since the night she discovered who Malcolm truly was, and she hated that for the second time, Malcolm's decision to withhold information, to omit certain truths, had forced her to stumble upon it herself, increasing the impact of the truth tenfold. Perhaps the anger she still felt towards him had partially motivated her phone call to Detective Duncan. A small act of revenge, of which Malcolm would never know. Her own secret to keep. But mostly, she wanted someone to talk to. She wanted someone who didn't omit truths, someone for whom she did not have to wear a brave face.

It hadn't been easy to arrange. Since the murder of their friends, and the attempt on Malcolm's life, he insisted she had round the clock security in place. There were now two men permanently by her side, and the only brief moments of freedom she felt were while she showered or went to the bathroom. It was necessary, she knew, but that didn't change the fact that it was suffocating. The fact that she had lived in a fish bowl most of her marriage had done nothing to prepare her for this. The police usually just sat outside the house eating fast food, or occasionally tailed her car to the shopping centre. They had never once knocked on the bathroom door while she was urinating to check she was alright, nor had they gone through her dry cleaning to check for bombs or bugs. It was infuriating, and only added to the resentment she felt for Malcolm at that moment.

She sent the detective a text, afraid a phone conversation would be over heard: Detective, would like to accept your kind offer of assistance. Could we meet? Marie Carter. He responded within seconds with a coffee shop address, suggesting they meet there the following day. But her 'body guards' for that day were unknown to Marie, and she couldn't guarantee they would keep the meeting a secret. She would have to wait a couple of days for Mickey to come on duty. She trusted him implicitly, and knew he would never tell Malcolm if she asked him not to. After years of him driving her, and watching over her, she felt like he was family. She recalled the conversation as she waited for the detective to arrive.

"Mickey, I need you to do something for me."

"Yes Mrs. Carter, you know I would do anything for you."

"Do you remember the detective who came to the house the other day?"

"Yes Mrs. Carter."

"I need to meet with him, but Malcolm can never know."

"Why?"

"I'm sure you know what's going on with this man Jonathan Savage; you know what happened to Richard and his family. I need to talk to the detective about that. But we would have to keep it a secret. Just you and me. Can you do that for me? Please? I wouldn't ask you if it wasn't important."

He looked so confused, so worried, as he thought this over for several minutes. Occasionally he would mutter to himself, as if he was debating what he should do in some kind of internal monologue. Eventually the muttering stopped and the confused look was replaced with resignation. "If I don't help you, you would go anyway, wouldn't you, except you would have to slip us guards to do it right?"

Marie was a little surprised he realised this. Mickey was not known for his intelligence. He was the perfect goon – he followed orders, never asked questions, and was built like a brick shit house. Yet he had just read her like a book. "Right."

He thought again for a moment. "Okay. I'll help you because that way I can still keep you safe, and I won't tell Mr. Carter if you don't want me to."

"Promise?"

"Cross my heart."

They decided to send the second guard, a man affectionately nicknamed 'The pit bull' by his peers, on a fool's errand for an hour, while Mickey watched out for Marie at the coffee shop. Pit bull was a tall, sallow faced man, who reminded Marie of Lurch from the Addams Family movies. He was brighter than Mickey, and had taken a bit of persuasion to collect the items on the list Marie provided, but Mickey's insistence that Marie would be safe with him and a crisp fifty-pound note had changed his mind. And so it was that Marie found herself sitting at the Cafe Rouge, sipping peppermint tea, wishing it was something stronger. Mickey sat at the back of the coffee shop, facing the front entrance.

He's late. Maybe he's not coming. She checked her phone and realised it was only four minutes after the hour. She began to get impatient anyway, knowing they only had an hour at best. She became aware of a tapping sound, and was mildly irritated until she realised it was the sound of her own foot tapping against the reclaimed wooden table leg. Why was she so nervous? It was hardly the first time she'd spoken to a police officer one on one. But this was different. He was different and she knew it.

She almost didn't notice him arriving. He slipped inside the door and shook the rain off his coat, his wet hair clinging to his forehead. He smiled when he saw her, weaving his way between the small tables and mismatched chairs. It was a cursory smile, made out of politeness rather than genuine happiness. Clearly he knew what she wished to discuss.

When he reached her table, she rose to greet him, and there was an awkward exchange as he went to hug her and she went to shake his hand, made all the more awkward when he caught sight of Mickey.

"He's my security. It's Malcolm's idea."

His face visibly flinched when she said his name. It was only fleeting, but she noticed it, nonetheless. "I see. Probably a good idea, considering......" He tailed off.

Considering what? Considering her husband was at war with a sociopath? Considering her friends had just been brutally murdered? There was no need to state the obvious, though. She had a target painted on her back, and they both knew it.

"I was surprised to get your text."

"I was surprised to write it."

For a moment they sat in awkward silence, neither sure how to broach the subject, both unsure what they could say, what they should say. While they sat, she listened to him breathing deeply, each exhalation almost a sigh. She didn't want to look him in the eye, so she studied the back of his hand placed on top of the table. He chewed his nails, and there was a black ink stain on his left index finger.

A mousey waitress approached them to take his order. He didn't seem to notice her flirt with him as he ordered an Americano.

"He told you then."

"Yes, he told me."

"Everything?"

"Everything."

He nodded, sighing heavily. He didn't even look at the waitress as she placed the cup down, despite her hovering just a second more than she needed to. He just stared into the dark, steaming liquid.

"Who is this guy? Why is he doing this?"

"You have to understand; Jonathan Savage is a different breed of criminal. He's evil."

"You mean more evil than my husband?"

He didn't answer, instead shifting uncomfortably in his seat. "I can't discuss your husband's case."

"I didn't call you to talk about my husband."

He looked up from his cup, and into her eyes, swallowing hard before speaking. "Why did you call me, Marie?"

It was the first time he'd ever called her by her first name. A fact that did not go unnoticed by either of them. They stared at one another a moment. She thought about lying to him, she certainly felt the urge to put her defenses back up. But she called him for a reason. She had gone to a considerable amount of trouble to ensure Malcolm wouldn't find out. There was no going back now.

"I called you because I'm afraid. I'm afraid of something happening to Malcolm, and I can't talk to him about it. I can't talk to him because he hid it from me, and because I don't want to heap my worries onto his own. I can't talk to him because he will try to reassure me instead of telling me how it is. I need someone to tell me how it is, to tell me what I should do. I don't know what to do."

She could feel herself welling up, a lump forcing its way into her throat. She remembered her friends. She saw little Elijah, she saw Malcolm's face contorted with pain, and before she could stop herself, a tear fell, making its way to her lips, the salty, warm taste all too familiar now.

He reached out to her, pausing briefly, before placing his hand on hers. She let it rest there a moment, finding comfort in its clammy warmth. Once she composed herself, she softly removed her hand from under his and placed it on her lap, feeling a little guilty for the intimate moment shared with a man other than her husband.

"I'm fine."

He looked a little disappointed, perhaps a little hurt. "What you should do, is leave."

"Malcolm would never...."

"Malcolm is going to get you killed. Both of you."

She was shocked, and felt herself becoming defensive. "Malcolm loves me. He'll protect me."

"If you really believed that, you wouldn't be here with me."

She didn't have an answer for that one.

"Look, you want someone to tell you the truth? Well here it is, Jonathan Savage is a sick fuck who has gotten away with raping and murdering at least four women, that we know of. He's implicated in dozens of homicides, none of which involved quick deaths, and I have no doubt he's been involved in dozens more. He's ruthless and sadistic and he has his sights set firmly on your husband's empire, and by association, you. Malcolm's had a long run at playing Don, longer than most, but he's old hat now, and Savage is gunning for his place at the top. If he knows what's good for him, if he cares about you AT ALL, he will cash in his assets and take you far, far away from here. That's how it is."

He slammed his fist onto the table to emphasise his point, and the mousey waitress was eyeing them suspiciously from the counter. Mickey was half out of his seat, looking to Marie for direction. She nodded at him, and he sat back down. She didn't know how to feel. After all, this was what she asked him here for, but that didn't make it any easier to hear.

A few more minutes passed. Another silence, this time not awkward, more resigned. She checked her watch. Time was almost up. She took a note from her purse and placed it on the table between them, resting it there. "Thank you, for being honest with me."

As she went to leave, he placed his hand on hers once more, this time more firmly, but still tender. "Please....be safe."

She thought for a moment that he was waiting to say something else, but he simply slid his hand off hers and walked away, leaving her alone with Mickey and the waitress.

Mickey rose to pull her chair out. "Did the copper upset you, Mrs. Carter?"

"No Mickey, he was just trying to help that's all."

He half smiled, clearly unsure about this, but didn't ask her anything more. As they walked to the car, she barely noticed the rain. She felt more confused than ever. Fraser was right, she knew that. Leaving was the obvious choice. But Malcolm was a proud man. He had bled and fought for his position, and he would never just give it up because of some young thug like Savage. Then there were his men. Men like Mickey. He would never just abandon them to Savage and his goons. To Malcolm, loyal employees like Mickey were family. That's why Richard's death was such a blow. It wasn't just the loss he felt, but the guilt that he didn't prevent it. Even if they did up sticks and leave, there was no guarantee Savage wouldn't track them down anyway. Given what she had learned about him so far, it didn't seem far-fetched. No, Malcolm would never just walk away, and she would never ask him to. If she did, he would drop everything, she knew that. But she loved him too much to ask him to give up everything he'd built. No, she made a vow, 'for better or worse', and she intended to keep it. But most surprisingly, Marie realised that not only would she not want him to run, but she may even feel a little ashamed if he did. She didn't marry the type of man who ran away. She married someone strong and brave. She married a fighter.

As these thoughts formed and reformed in her mind, she didn't notice that Pit Bull was standing across the road, lurking in the shadows of a narrow alleyway, watching her carefully. She hadn't noticed that he'd been there throughout the entire meeting, and she didn't notice him as he walked towards a car that pulled up nearby. A car with blacked out windows and reinforced glass. A car with her husband inside.

Chapter Fourteen
-Four Years Ago

The smile on Marie's face seemed to be a permanent feature these days; she couldn't help it. She felt like she was floating, a constant euphoria surrounded her as she floated through streets and passing faces. To passers-by, she must have looked like a grinning idiot, but the ring on her hand, the love in her heart, meant nothing, no one, could possibly burst this blissful bubble.

Every item of clothing she owned seemed to perfectly compliment the deep navy blue sapphires. Every kind of light seemed to make the diamonds sparkle and shine; a constellation of stars on her hand.

Since the engagement, they had been even more affectionate with one another, even more in love. Every hug, every kiss, was a promise of a million more to come, a lifetime's worth. Malcolm barely went to work, choosing to spend every waking moment with his betrothed. They spent days lying in bed together, making love, eating take-aways, laughing like fools. It was wonderful. It couldn't last that way forever of course. Malcolm had a lot of commitments; staff who needed paid, antiques which needed to be sourced and sold, books which needed to be balanced, but it was a beautiful time that reinforced their bond to each other. An unbreakable bond.

Today, he'd been called away on urgent business. A member of his staff had apparently been stealing from him, abusing a position of trust as Malcolm had put it, and he needed to be dealt with internally. Malcolm seemed extremely upset by it. Something she learned quickly from his interactions with his staff, and from what bits and pieces she picked up about his work – the loyalty of his employees was extremely important to him. He seemed to take any deviation from that loyalty extremely personally. As he got dressed in his grey pin striped suit, Marie tying his pale yellow, silk tie in a perfect Windsor knot (she'd become quite proficient at this over the course of their relationship), she could see growing irritation, the impatience to confront this staff member, in the constant agitated shuffle of his feet, the unnecessary checking and rechecking of his watch.

"Sweetheart, don't let it get to you so much. These things happen, in every business."

"I know; I just hate dealing with such things. Especially when it's someone in whom I placed a certain level of trust, of responsibility. I'm..." He paused, as if he was searching for the right word to describe how he felt in that moment. "I'm disappointed, that's all. Very disappointed."

"Don't let it ruin your day. Go do the whole HR bit and get it sorted internally, and then hand his ass over to the police. Let them sort him out."

He stopped shuffling and stared at her, his lips parted with a word hanging just on their edges. For a moment Marie felt like he wanted to tell her something important, something he was clearly reluctant to say. But almost as quickly as those silent words tried to escape his mouth, they disappeared again. His lips closed into a smile, then a kiss.

"He'll be dealt with." And with that he was gone, determinedly marching out of the bedroom.

She decided to go for a run. The weather was crisp and cool, perfect for such activity, and the thought of a wedding dress fitting suddenly looming in her future inspired sudden action. After months of Malcolm's breakfasts in bed and home cooking, she noticed her figure getting distinctly soft around the edges. Of course, Malcolm dismissed her worries, pulling her onto the bed and declaring just how stunning she was as he kissed those soft edges, but Marie wasn't entirely convinced. She wanted to look her very best, and that would mean fewer pancakes and more exercise.

It had been months since she'd done any real exercise, and the heavy breathing and sweating which quickly ensued as she left the house, along with her ever reddening face, made that perfectly obvious to both Marie and any passer-by who cared to pay attention to her. She barely squeezed into her Lycra bottoms, and her trainers were definitely on their last legs, but with the aid of a great play list, as recommended by Sara's beloved DJ Charlie, she quickly found her rhythm again.

It was on days like these that Marie loved London. The bright early morning sunshine cast the buildings in a happy, welcoming light, and as was the case with all indigenous residents of the United

Kingdom, any sign of sunshine, however minor and even when accompanied with biting temperatures, was met with the happiest of smiles and the warmest of embraces. Everyone she passed was bright, and some had even attempted to expose their bare skin to this crevice of light amongst the all too often grey and drizzly days, with plenty of legs and arms on display, goose pimpled but happy to be free of their clothing prisons.

After the first few kilometres, she could feel herself getting out of breath and decided to take a short break at a small children's play park. The metal bench, covered in graffiti, was cold against her now warm, perspiring body, and it gave her a small amount of relief as she caught her breath again. Nearby, small children screamed and chased each other, or played on the swings trying to go as high and as fast as they could.

Their smiles were infectious and Marie couldn't help but imagine what their children would look like. She hoped if they had a son, he would have his father's good looks, his kindness and charm. She pictured a tiny version of Malcolm, wearing an identical grey pin striped suit and silk yellow tie, and she laughed out loud. It was something they had discussed since the engagement; having a family. It seemed natural when two people were as happy as they were, as in love, to increase that love, that happiness, with the addition of another into their circle. A child was something Marie always wanted.

In a way, it would be her way of undoing her own childhood, of proving these things weren't cyclical. Her way of breaking the pattern. She would have a child and she would show it nothing but love and affection. She would tell it every day how special and perfect it was. She would love it with all her heart, they both would, and with that she would prove her parents wrong. She would show them how it should be done. She remembered her grandmother, and suddenly felt sad this imagined child would never meet her. But she realised that she would be her inspiration, her example of how to treat her children, and in that sense, she would play a vital part. She smiled at this thought, watching the children play their games. Their laughter carrying on the cool breeze.

After many minutes passed, her mind drifting between memories and an imagined future, she eventually came back to the present. She bent down and re-tied her laces as she read some of the hand-scrawled words strewn along every inch of the bench. Some were declarations of love, or as close to them as the younger generation got these days, the likes of 'Paul and Chantelle 4ever' and 'Macy luvs Stevo' scrawled in black sharpie. It was hardly poetry. There was the odd phone number offering a 'good time', an unnecessarily detailed drawing of an ejaculating penis, and an obligatory swastika amongst the many messages. Nothing overly surprising. The only one which caught her eye amongst the scribbles and symbols was a neatly written quote on the far right arm of the bench. It read: 'You are free to choose. But you are not free from the consequence of your choice.' A Universal Paradox. Marie thought about this only briefly, before she pulled herself away from the cold embrace of the bench, from her thoughts and memories, and began her march again. A steady march towards her choices, and their consequences.

Chapter Fifteen
-Present Day

Fraser checked his watch and immediately realised it was less than forty seconds since he last checked it. It was like a nervous twitch, something he had to do in order to feel the smallest bit of reassurance. She was late. He checked his phone for what must have been the fifth time since he sat down inside the coffee shop. There were no texts, no messages stating their meeting was cancelled. He was half pleased and half worried by this. She always texted or left him a voicemail if she was unable to make their clandestine meetings, because Malcolm had suddenly come home early or she couldn't ditch her second security guard. His mind always went to the worst case scenario; what if she was hurt? What if she was taken? Perhaps it was the cop in him. After years of crime scenes and crying loved ones, he had learned to expect the worst and hope for the best. But lately, as the violence escalated, as the murder rate soared in the Capital to an all-time high, his hope was waning and the worst case scenario seemed to be the only scenario. He checked his watch again.

He didn't know why he felt compelled to protect Marie, to save her from Malcolm, from herself, he just knew he had to do something, anything. If he could save one life, stop one killing, it would all be worth it, right? The sleepless nights, the constant overtime, the station showers and naps at his desk being his only rest these days. This job had always been hard, lonely even, but lately, since the gang war started, it felt as if he lived at the police station, and in truth, he felt lonelier than ever. He had dated a good few girls in his day, some more serious than others, but relationships were difficult to maintain in his line of work. When he dated fellow police officers, it felt like all they talked about, all they had in common, was the job. And when he dated civilians, he was nagged and guilt tripped after every missed dinner date or forgotten anniversary. They could never understand, with their nine to five lives, why he was being held on AGAIN or why he couldn't commit to attending a cousin's wedding on a certain date, because he wouldn't necessarily have his rest day off. It was impossible. His meetings with Marie made him feel that little bit less lonely. She was the best of both worlds; a civilian who understood his job. He had begun to think of her as a friend, not just a name in a file. He noticed her thaw towards him too, becoming a little friendlier, more relaxed with every conversation. He knew she was lonely too. She'd moved here from another country, just like him, and had few friends as a result. On top of that, Malcolm's world was a closed circle, it had to be for security, more so now than ever before, and after losing Linda and her infant son, her circle had become even smaller. Their mutual loneliness created a bond.

But it was more than that; Marie needed him.

He could see the path she was headed on, and the outcome was never going to be good. Even if everything suddenly changed for the better, and the war was over, Marie would still be married to a murderer, she would still be under the control of that man. And if Savage got hold of her; he couldn't even think about it, the prospect was too horrible. He checked his watch again. Where was she?

He was just opening the address book on his phone as she walked in, her face flushed and glowing. She looked like she had been running. He stood and pulled her chair out for her to sit.

"I'm so sorry, but I could not get away from my shadows, not even for a second to call you. In the end I just ditched them. I couldn't stand being babysat a second longer."

She began to laugh, at a joke as yet unspoken. He loved her laugh; it was unapologetically loud. Sadly, he didn't hear it as often as he would like these days. After a minute of giggling to herself, stopping only briefly to order a green tea, she regaled him with her adventure of escape through a cramped bathroom window in a crowded bar, only to find herself trapped in a fenced yard. It had taken three goes to climb onto a bin and over one of the fences. She practically ran to the coffee shop.

Fraser laughed with her. He was flattered she went to so much effort to see him. "Those two shadows of yours are probably frantic right about now."

"Let them be, they were infuriating me. One even tried to walk in to my Gynae appointment this morning, for God's sake. It's getting to the point of ridiculousness."

They both laughed again, but this time it faded, as the unsaid hung before them. They both knew why these men were becoming more and more enthusiastic about their roles, and why she had security in the first place. Things were getting worse out there, they both knew it.

"How do you do it? Your job. How do you stand it?"

He was taken aback for a moment. After a dozen conversations now, after several meetings and stolen phone calls, this was the first time she had asked him about his job. They would talk about Savage, yes, about the threat at hand, but the fact that he was a police officer was never mentioned, deliberately so on Marie's side. Or so it had appeared to Fraser, as if she needed to pretend so she felt less guilty about their friendship, less like she was betraying her husband by meeting with the enemy.

Then there was the question itself; how do you answer that? There were the usual responses; to help people, to protect and serve, but he knew they would never satisfy Marie, and he knew to an extent that they weren't true. Of course he wanted to help people; why else would you become a cop? But truthfully, that wasn't why he joined and it wasn't why he stayed. "That's not easy to answer. Sometimes, I find myself asking that same question. The truth is, a long time ago, I let someone down, I let my dad down. When things were bad, instead of fighting through it, I gave up. I became someone I hated, and in doing so I spat in the face of everything he stood for, of everything he had ever raised me to be. I guess I joined because I wanted to make him proud again, to be the man he raised me to be, a good man, like him. I don't know, I can't explain it any better than that."

He looked down at his now empty cup, the dark staining of what used to be coffee marking the edges. He suddenly felt embarrassed. They had talked about their respective pasts, and she knew about his father, about his childhood, but he'd told her those things in more of a factual, getting to know someone kind of way. He had never been this open or emotional about those events. He didn't tend to discuss his feelings so openly.

He felt her hand move onto his, as it still clutched at the coffee cup's edges. It was soft and warm, and he could smell the faintest hint of rose water hand lotion. At first, he didn't want to look up, but the silence had gone on too long now. Eventually he would have to re-join the conversation. Slowly his eyes met hers. She was gazing at him warmly, fondly even, just waiting until he was ready.

"I understand. I understand completely."

Chapter Sixteen
-Four Years Ago

Organising the wedding was bittersweet. There were so many wonderful moments, like the day Malcolm and she ate cake samples until they felt physically sick, or bridesmaid dress shopping with Sara. But it was all tainted with sadness and haunted by ghosts from her past, of the people who wouldn't be there, people who couldn't be there. She hadn't even noticed it at first, it had crept in so slowly; she simply pushed the thoughts to the back of her mind, but eventually it became impossible to ignore.

The first time these feelings really hit her, was the moment of the 'big reveal'. It was the fourth dress shop they'd been to, the tenth dress she tried on, and the moment the shop assistant buttoned up the back, she knew she found 'the dress'. It was stunning – made of antique ivory lace, it hugged her figure tightly, before it opened out into a long, graceful train. The sweetheart neckline of the corset, the pearl buttons – it was everything she wanted in one dress, and it made her feel like Grace Kelly. Her choice was validated as she exited the changing room to gasps of admiration from Sara, Mickey and the rest of the staff.

"Oh my god Marie! I've never seen you look so beautiful!"

Marie was surprised to see tears welling up in Sara's eyes; she was the least soppy person she'd ever known. When Charlie had proposed to her, at a candlelit dinner in a very romantic French bistro, she laughed at him thinking he was joking around; it had been a rather awkward moment for Marie, Malcolm and all of Sara and Charlie's friends, who unbeknownst to her, were waiting to jump out and yell 'surprise' once she accepted. They all laughed about it now, but Charlie looked mortified at the time. "You look just like Grandma when she got married!"

Marie smiled and stared at her reflection while Sara held up different veils. I do look like her. And that's when it hit her, the fact that her grandmother wouldn't see her walk down the aisle. It was such a silly thing to get upset about; after all, she'd been gone a long time; it wasn't a fresh wound, but it pained her nonetheless. And then there was the fact that, apart from Sara, she would have no family there. She hadn't spoken to her parents in so long, and after years of such an unhappy home, such a dysfunctional family life, she had been happy with that arrangement. But every little girl pictured their father walking them down the aisle, their mother offering words of wisdom. It broke her heart a little to know they wouldn't be there, even though she knew the image of the mother and father she so desperately wanted, she had always yearned for, didn't exist.

She hadn't spoken to her parents since she moved out, and she barely thought of them since she moved to London. As for her siblings, she'd never been close to them; her brother was in and out of jail most of her life, her sister cut contact with them when she married her husband, a man who considered himself above their kind. Their family was a fractured, dysfunctional one, a fact that always pained Marie. She vowed that when she had children, she would tell them every day how much she loved them, she would provide the home she had always wanted, but never had, one filled with love and laughter.

"Are you okay? Marie....are you okay?"

She must have been staring into that mirror for quite a while, because she suddenly realised the shop staff, Mickey and Sara were all staring at her. "Yes, I'm fine. I'll take it." She smiled a half smile, which seemed to satisfy the staff, who began to type things into the computer and discuss delivery dates and fittings with each other. Sara, however, looked like she would require further reassurance.

"Are you sure you're okay?"

"Yes, I was just lost in thought for a moment, that's all."

She seemed to understand without Marie having to say anything. Sara could be so intuitive sometimes. "She's still here you know. She's watching over us, I really believe that! And I know she would never approve of you being all sad, especially on a day like this! You're getting married Marie!"

"I'm getting married! You're right, I'm fine, honestly. Would you go grab me some shoes to try on with this dress?"

Sara kissed her on the cheek and hugged her tightly for just a moment. "I'm on it."

After Sara shuffled off to the other side of the

store with various members of the staff, Marie was left alone, staring into the large mirror. There was a crack on the bottom right hand corner which she had only just noticed. We all have cracks; we all have flaws.

"Miss?"

She jumped a little; she'd forgotten Mickey was there, holding their bags and coats. He'd driven Marie to every printer, every caterer, and every dress shop since she started planning the wedding. He had tried the cake samples, carried the dresses, and smelled the flowers without any complaint. In fact, he was rather good at it and helped immeasurably, at one point talking her out of the purple bridesmaid dress she was leaning towards. Something for which she was now extremely grateful. Marie even began to call him her very own best man.

"She's right you know."

"Sorry?"

"Miss Sara, she's right." Despite her best efforts, Mickey still referred to them both as Miss.

"Right about what?"

"I didn't mean to listen, but she's right about your grandma. I mean, I don't believe in God or nothing, but I do believe people live on, in our memories of them and our love for them, you know what I mean? Like, when she had children, and they had you, a little piece of her passed on and it will keep going when you have babies as well. Her love for you made you who you are, and it will shape how you raise your kids and treat other people kindly, like you do me, and so you see, she's not really gone at all. She's still here, in you. Does that make sense?"

Marie could feel herself welling up, her vision

becoming blurred by the tears forming on her eyelashes.

"Oh Miss, I'm sorry. I didn't want to upset you; I was trying to help is all."

"You did help Mickey, you did, Thank you." She hugged him as best she could, but he was so broad she could barely get her arms around him.

He placed his hand on her head. "You don't need to worry about absent family Miss, because you got a new one right here."

She squeezed a little tighter. She hadn't realised before just how important Mickey was to her. He was always there, always ready to help, and not just because it was his job. He was there for her in ways far beyond his job description.

She raised her head from his large chest. "Mickey, would you walk me down the aisle?"

He looked at her wide eyed, his smile growing across his face, his chest swelling with so much pride she thought he would burst. "It would be my honour, Miss."

Chapter Seventeen
-Present Day

The guilt from her friendship with Fraser was beginning to overtake the worry she felt, but the stolen phone calls and the brief meetings were the only moments of relief she felt at this turbulent time. Since that evening in the office, Malcolm had begun to pull away from her. He was always at the club, always having meetings, and the few times he was at home, he was withdrawn and distant. She even began to notice a visible change, the stress clearly taking its toll. She couldn't blame him, or be mad. She could only imagine what was going on in his mind, but she missed the man she married. There were brief moments when he would appear; a soft kiss when he thought she was sleeping, a squeeze of her hand, but mostly he retreated from her, and that hurt her deeply. She tried at first to reassure him in any way she could, but it seemed to make it all harder for him, as if her affection was a reminder of exactly what he could lose if he failed.

And so she sought comfort from Fraser. He was always so kind to her, but most importantly, so completely honest. He would tell her how the battle appeared to be going, or how many losses each side had suffered. He would discuss the threat of Savage candidly. However, she noticed he would very deliberately never mention Malcolm. He said it was for data protection, but she felt the reason was more personal than that, as if he hated to acknowledge her husband's existence.

After a while, the conversations began to turn away from these current events and became more personal, intimate even. They discussed everything from their childhoods to their favourite books and movies. Over time, Fraser had become less of a source of information or sounding board for her fears to more like something resembling a friend.

He'd grown up in Edinburgh, part of a large Catholic family of four brothers and two sisters. They were extremely poor, but very happy. His mother was a school teacher. A kind woman, who whistled while she cleaned and loved to bake. His father was a second generation police officer who had bestowed on Fraser a sense of justice and the importance of doing the right thing. He was thirteen years old when his father ran into a burning building to save a young boy. When the building collapsed, so did Fraser's world. His mother, unable to keep up with the mortgage payments, was forced to give up their home and move to his grandparents' in Dundee. She couldn't find a job there, and so she retreated inside herself, unable to cope with such a loss, even for the sake of her children. She stopped whistling, then washing, and eventually eating, the depression taking hold of her completely. Within a year, the woman she had been disappeared completely, to the point that no one, not even Fraser, was surprised when they found her car in that small patch of woods, a hose pipe attached to the exhaust.

He began to blame his father for everything – if only he hadn't gone into the building, if he hadn't tried to act the hero, then everything would still be good, just like the old days. As a teenager, he coped the only way he knew how, by rebelling. He began to hang out with a local gang of troublemakers, he experimented with drugs and alcohol, attempting to numb his feelings and simultaneously to become someone completely opposite from his father. The man who had chosen the life of a stranger over his own family.

At sixteen, he ended up back in Edinburgh, living in a dingy squat with a handful of other runaways. With stealing the only way to eat, he resigned himself to becoming a criminal, to living on the outside of society. One night he was caught by a shop owner, stealing a loaf of bread and a bottle of vodka. The officer who attended had worked with his father, and after paying for the goods himself and arranging for Fraser to clean the shop as penance, he took Fraser under his wing and steered him in the right direction. Four years later, he graduated from the Scottish Police College in Kincardine, with his siblings and surviving grandparent cheering him on.

Fraser was a dedicated and hardworking officer, partly because he was trying to re-write past wrongs, and partly because he wanted so desperately to make his father proud, honestly believing he was there somewhere, watching over him. After five years as a beat cop he joined the Criminal Investigation Department, working initially in the Burglary team before moving to Murder Investigation. His first case was a series of murders believed to be linked to the modern day gangster Malcolm Carter and his band of merry thugs.

But, Fraser didn't tell her everything. His first day on the job, he was briefed on the basics; the pictures of the main players, the rap sheets and known associates, the mountains of paperwork amassed over years of investigations, some fruitful, some not. And so it was that whilst conducting this investigation, and reading through the boxes upon boxes of files and papers, he discovered Marie. It was like something out of a novel really – a beautiful, naïve young woman taken in by the charm of a monster. After months of reading transcripts from her previous interviews, and listening to the tapes from wire taps, he decided he had to save her, to rescue her from the Beast. He hadn't meant to fall in love with her. He convinced himself that the reason he had a special interest in her, the reason he had worn out the edges of a surveillance photograph of her and read and re-read her file, was because he was concerned for her, because she needed his help. When he asked her to come in for questioning that day, he'd been nervous. He told himself it was just because this was his first big case, but he knew better. He knew it was because he was afraid she wouldn't live up to the image he created of her in his head, a jigsaw made up of all the snippets of information he had access to. But she had lived up to it, and more. She was intelligent and brave, but vulnerable, and so much more beautiful in person than any photograph could have ever portrayed.

That meeting only cemented his determination to save her. The surveillance photo, a grainy black and white image of Marie laughing, was removed from the boxes of files and placed in the top drawer of his desk. A reminder of why he was working so late, why he hadn't slept properly in months. Inspiration to keep him going when it all got too much.

But after months of killing himself, he was no closer to putting Malcolm behind bars. He was just too careful, too intelligent. Malcolm Carter had been mentioned in the file of at least two dozen murders over the length of his reign, and there had never even been enough evidence to interview him. Previous officers in charge of the case had been inspired by Eliot Ness, the American FBI agent who took down Al Capone on tax charges, but Malcolm had ensured that every T was crossed and i dotted, and not a single penny was found to be out of place. In fact, Malcolm found their efforts so amusing he changed the name of his bar as a reminder that he is truly the Untouchable.

When Jonathan Savage appeared on the scene, Fraser was almost relieved. He'd set his sights firmly on Malcolm, and if the police couldn't take Malcolm down, at least Savage might. But that relief soon turned to fear as it became clear that not only was Jonathan a sociopathic monster, but that Marie was also in his cross hairs. Fraser never thought he would be in the position where Malcolm would be considered by law enforcement as the lesser of two evils, but after attending the scene of four of Jonathan's victims in just a three-week period, there was no doubt that that's how things stood.

And so, after another stolen phone call, Marie sat on a bench in Hyde Park staring at The Serpentine. She watched the droplets of rain splash onto the murky lake, sending ripples dancing along the surface. She thought about Jonathan Savage, about the ripples he had caused to her world, and she shivered. Lost in thought, Marie did not hear Fraser approach, only noticing him when he rested his hand gently on her shoulder. She returned his touch, resting her hand a moment on his as he came around the bench and sat beside her. He looked so tired, with blood shot eyes and sallow skin. Marie could see more than a few restless nights etched on his face.

"You're late."

"I know, I'm sorry. I thought I was being followed."

"What? By who?"

"I wasn't, it's fine. I think this whole thing.... I think it's starting to get to me, that's all. I wasn't."

Marie felt like he was trying to convince himself more than her, but she pushed those worries down and told herself it was fine. She had become more and more practised at that of late. An expert in denial.

"Have there been more murders?"

He didn't answer. Marie learned early on that silence from Fraser spoke louder than any words.

"Savage?"

He closed his eyes tight, and looked away from her towards the trees. She knew exactly what Fraser was working on these past few weeks. After Malcolm's revelations in the study, she began to read newspapers again. They were hard not to notice, with their fear-mongering headlines written in big, bold black letters, and the photographs of men in SOCO suits and blue police cordon tape plastered across every front page. Bloody battle for London continues, The Streets of London run red with blood, Body parts found in local playground. The list went on and on. This war was raging all around her, and she could feel the enemy closing in.

"He wants me, doesn't he?"

He stood up, taking a hurried step away from her, where he paused a moment, his palms resting on his forehead, as if the thought he was forming was painful. Suddenly he spun around, getting down on his haunches so he faced her now, his hands grasping hers tightly. "Do you trust me?"

"What?"

"Do you trust me Marie? It's a simple question." He seemed so agitated, a little manic even. It scared her.

"Yes."

"Then leave with me.... tonight."

She stared at him, unsure what to say, almost afraid to respond. "I can't just...."

"Of course you can. I have money, savings, I can get you out of here. Get you somewhere safe."

"But Malcolm...."

"Fuck Malcolm. Fuck him. If he wants to get himself killed that's his prerogative, but you don't have to die with him, Marie. If anything happened to you...."

"Why are you saying this?" She wrenched her hands free, surprised at his strength.

"Because Malcolm's pride is going to get you both killed. Because I have seen exactly what Savage is capable of in all its bloody glory, painted all over walls and floors." He was shouting now, his voice echoing around the empty park, "Because I cannot stand by while you become another victim, another statistic. But mostly, because I love you. Because I've always loved you. Marie, Please......"

He reached his hand to her cheek, and she leaned away, rising from the bench to stand opposite him. She was in shock, her head reeling with the revelation. Her mind raced at one hundred miles a minute, with every emotion and thought crashing together all at once. She struggled to form a simple declarative sentence amongst this internal chaos. "I'm married."

"To a murderer, Marie. To a scumbag criminal who fancies himself the Godfather. I know this is hard to hear, I know you don't want to believe it, but that's the truth. He lied to you. He's always lied to you. But it's okay, you didn't know. He manipulated you; I've seen cases like this a million times. You don't have to live like this Marie, no matter what he's made you think, no matter how much he controls you. There is help. I can help. I love you, please let me save you."

He stepped towards her again, reaching out to her, but she pushed him back, harder than she intended and with more force than he expected. He looked visibly shocked, as if he was totally unprepared for any kind of rejection.

"Is that what you think I am? Some naive little girl, swept away by a flashy suit and a charming smile?"

"I just...."

"You just what, Fraser? You just want to save me? That's what you said wasn't it, save me? I don't need to be saved, not from my marriage. I love

Malcolm, I have always loved him. I never said otherwise to you, I never once said to you I wanted anyone else but him."

He looked wounded, tears welling in his eyes. Marie might have pitied him if she wasn't so angry. "You don't know what he is. If you did, you would understand why I am trying to help you."

"Oh but I do know. I've always known."

The wounded puppy look on his face slowly gave way to confusion. He stood staring at her, like he was trying desperately to will her to change her mind, to say something, anything else. "I don't understand."

"I'm not some gullible little girl living in denial, Fraser. I found out years ago exactly what Malcolm does for a living. In fact, I walked in on him in action, I saw the blood and the violence and I stayed. I stayed. I went into this marriage with my eyes open. If I had wanted to leave Malcolm, don't you think I would have done it then? I don't need to be rescued. I don't need to be saved. I am exactly where I want to be, and I always have been."

He seemed to be searching for words, his jaw trembling now, his image of Marie shattering like glass. "I'm in love with you." He said it so quietly, Marie could barely make it out.

"If I ever gave you the impression I had romantic feelings towards you then I'm sorry, I truly am. The truth is, I needed a friend, you were my friend...." She choked up, tears rising in her throat, the sudden realisation of what she had just lost.

Fraser couldn't stand to see her in pain. He wanted so desperately to show her the love he felt, the love he believed with all his heart was more worthy than anything Malcolm Carter could produce. He pulled her towards him, and kissed her, their lips meeting only briefly before Marie pulled away.

They stood in silence a moment, broken only by the sound of their heavy breathing, by the sound of the rain, getting heavier now, as if the weather was reacting to how she felt in that moment. When she gathered herself enough to walk away from Fraser, from their friendship, she picked her bag up from the bench, and started towards the car which would take her home, back to Malcolm. Back to the life she had chosen. It may not be perfect, but it's mine. After two or three steps, she looked back at him. He was standing by the edge of the water, his head lowered, his arms hanging by his side, with fists clenched in frustration and disappointment. He didn't look at her, even as she spoke.

"Goodbye, Detective Duncan."

Chapter Eighteen
-Four Years Ago

As a young couple in love, planning to spend the rest of their lives together, the topic had come up, on more than one occasion. How many, what type, names had all been discussed as an inevitable eventuality, as something they both desired 'some day' but that was not necessarily on the immediate agenda. It was something they both looked forward to, both yearned for. A child, imagined at that time, felt as real to them as any other. Losing their baby had been truly devastating for them both.

She hadn't realised she was pregnant. Planning the wedding took up so much of her time. Her diary was filled with dress fittings and cake tasting, her thoughts were a jumble of vows and fantasies of what married life would be, something was bound to slip through. When she began vomiting, and feeling weak and dizzy, she assumed she had the flu. With all the running around she'd been doing, it was understandable that her immune system and body would suffer a little. She stayed in bed, dosed up on cold and flu medication, nursing a hot water bottle against her cramping stomach. She told herself the silver lining was getting this out of her system before the big day, but after days, it seemed to be getting worse instead of better.

Malcolm had been wonderful - staying home to tend to her, making her soup she couldn't keep down, reading to her. After three days, despite her protestations, he arranged for the doctor to visit that evening. "You're worrying too much."

"I'm going to be your husband. It's my job to worry and to take care of you."

When Sara visited that morning with a care basket, the clear concern she felt was written all over her. Marie made her best attempt at smiling, to reassure herself as much as Sara, but her stomach cramps were now so painful that she struggled not to cry out as she attempted to sit up.

"Jesus Marie, maybe you should go to the hospital. You look awful."

Charming and tactful as ever. "I'm fine, it's just a flu or something. The doctor is coming today."

The look on Sara's face clearly portrayed her dissatisfaction with the response. She reached her hand over and placed it on Marie's forehead, almost immediately withdrawing it, as if that slight touch had been enough to scold her; a bare hand on a hot stove. "Are you sure you're okay? You're boiling hot, Marie."

"Yes. It's this hot water bottle, that's all." She looked at her dubiously. After days of Mickey and Malcolm fussing around her like nurse maids, Marie couldn't take another person treating her like some porcelain doll. "How are you and Charlie getting on with the wedding plans without me?"

Her blatant ploy worked. Sara's face suddenly shifted from concern to excitement and she began regaling Marie with ideas for designing her own dress and the great band she was going to hire. But as quickly as the shift came, it left again, as she trailed off mid-way through an anecdote about her battle with Charlie to get him in some kind of suit. Suddenly, they sat in silence, as Sara simply stared at her engagement ring, twirling it around her slender finger. Marie watched her a moment, she was biting her bottom lip, something she did when she had to deliver bad news. Marie called it her 'tell'. "What is it?"

"He's been offered an amazing job, a residency in a world famous nightclub. It's a huge opportunity, but it's in Ibiza. We are staying for your wedding, I insisted he push the date back until after that, but we need to leave the next day."

Marie felt pain inside her chest, almost matching the pain in her abdomen. Sara had been her rock for so long, her entire family, and the only real friend she'd ever had besides Malcolm. It was going to be devastating to lose her, but she was happy Sara had found her own adventure, and she could see just how happy Charlie made her. She couldn't be selfish. "I'll miss you."

"No you won't, you'll visit me every summer for a wild party in the sun, and I'll come see you every Christmas! Promise me?"

"I promise!"

They embraced once more, but this time, Marie cried out in pain. Sara felt her forehead, the fever radiating from her even worse than a few moments before. Marie clutched her stomach, and Sara felt along it gently, as she flinched and winced with the pain of even this light gesture. Her stomach was rock hard, and Sara knew immediately something was very wrong. She quickly moved towards the door. "I'm just going to get Malcolm. Everything is going to be fine."

Marie realised she was biting her bottom lip as she spoke.

Chapter Nineteen
-Present Day

Marie gazed out of the car window, the rain so heavy now it obscured everything outside. She changed her focus, checking her reflection against the dreary grey backdrop of a London winter. It wasn't much better. Her eyeliner had run, snaking its way down her cheeks, and her lipstick was smudged from Fraser's desperate kiss. She suddenly felt embarrassed, using her sleeve to wipe her face, combing her hair with her fingers. The truth was she didn't know what else to do, she felt so helpless. Her appearance, her body, was about the only thing she had control over now, and it was betraying her through bloodshot, teary eyes and quivering lips. She had to stay strong.

A hand reached in from the front passenger seat, clasping a handkerchief. It was offered up with only an understanding half smile and a quick squeeze of her fingers as she reached for it.

"Thank you, Mickey."

He pointed out a roadworks sign to Pitbull, who had the privilege of driving today. After a brief debate about which route to take, it all went quiet again, only the metallic sound of the rain beating against the roof breaking the silence.

She'd been so angry at first, at Fraser, at Malcolm, at this ridiculous situation. But by the time she reached the car, that had given way to defeat and self-pity. She didn't have the energy to be mad anymore, she just wanted it all to go back to the way it was before. Before Savage.

There was a dull pop, and the car began to shudder slightly. "Shit. I think we have a puncture." Pitbull pulled into a side street, yanking the hand brake on. "Grab the jack, Mickey, I'll assess the damage." And with that he got out, slamming the door behind him.

Mickey opened the door too, using it as an anchor to drag his giant frame out of the lowered car. He popped his head back inside, as he held the door open. "Don't worry Miss, we'll sort it out in no..." He never got to finish the sentence. His face suddenly and inexplicably contorted with pain as he fell and crumpled beside the car.

She felt panic rise inside her. "Mickey?" She went to open the door, only to have it wrenched by some invisible force outside. She instinctively backed away into the opposite corner, as a black figure appeared, reaching for her, grabbing at her. She brought her knees to her chest, trying to make herself as small as possible. He was wearing a black mask over the lower half of his face, with a white jaw bone and bare teeth painted on it, giving the terrifying impression in the quickly fading light that the bottom half of his face was devoid of flesh. He grabbed at her, wrapping his fingers tight around her leg, and forcefully dragging her towards the open door. She unfolded under the force of his pull as she desperately clung to the opposite door handle. His gloves were wet, and as she pulled herself away from him, she felt his grip slide and loosen slightly. Taking advantage of the moment, she kicked out at his face with her free foot, hard enough to feel bone cracking underneath, before yanking her other leg free. She heard him howl in pain as she pushed the other door open, throwing herself out into the cold. She could hear footsteps behind her. Every time her feet hit the road, sending water up around them, she heard a corresponding thump behind her as the attacker closed his distance. Keep going, don't look back!

She began to scream, no words, just a loud and continuous scream, before she felt something hit her from behind, forcing her down hard onto the tarmac. She heard a crack, and felt pain shoot up her right arm as she attempted to break her fall. Her pursuer had tackled her to the ground, and was now on top of her, grabbing her hands and attempting to pin her down as she flailed and clawed at his face, partially tearing his mask off, this one identical to the last, except the skeletal grimace glowed green, creating an even more horrifying image in the closing darkness. She tried everything to break free, but her legs were trapped beneath the weight of his body, and eventually despite her efforts, he grabbed hold of both her arms, with one of his pinning them against her chest. He then used his free hand to grasp her hair, yanking it off the pavement before slamming it back down.

Everything began to swim and blur around her, and she felt her body going limp, her limbs no longer receiving the message to fight. Darkness began to close, and she felt herself falling into it, her brain desperately trying to shut down and reboot as she fought unconsciousness. The weight holding her down suddenly disappeared, and she blinked hard, attempting to focus on what was happening. She could see glimpses of the world amongst the darkness. She saw the man with the white mask slumped against the car, not moving. Near to him was another black mass, folded and crumpled, the dead eyes of Pitbull staring back at her. She turned her head with great effort to see the man with the green glowing mask wrestling with someone. She could hear yelling but it sounded so far away, as if she was down a long tunnel with only the rushing of blood ringing in her ears. She felt the darkness calling her to sleep, but she fought to stay conscious, using all of her energy to roll onto her side. She tried desperately to make her body sit up, to run, but no matter how much she concentrated, every limb seemed so heavy, every thought so delayed. Everything was in slow motion. She stared hard at the black figures and realised what was happening. Mickey? He was alive, and he was fighting to save her. She tried to scream again, to call out to him, but nothing came out.

The bulky figure of Mickey went still underneath the other body, and she caught glimpses of silver as the street light caught the edge of a knife, as it was plunged over and over downwards, into Mickey's lifeless body. No, Please No. She dragged herself forward, reaching out towards his hand, now lying limp beside his face, his eyes staring at her but not seeing her. She let herself lie beside him, staring into those eyes, wide with fear. She could hear him wheezing now, taking what she knew were his last breaths. He moved his hand slightly towards her, with obvious effort, as she moved her face to meet it. He stared at her a moment, a tear falling from his eye. She tried to speak, tried to tell him how much she loved him, how much he meant to her, how he had been her family, her truest, dearest friend. But instead, only a wail came out. A wail which sounded so foreign to Marie's ears that she barely recognised it as coming from her, only the ache in her throat as it was released being proof it was her voice; the cry of a dying animal. Slowly, the life left his eyes. She felt the already weak hold of his hand release and she knew he was gone. The grief was like nothing she'd ever felt before. It was soul crushing, overwhelming. It choked her as she struggled to breathe, to stay awake. Mickey. Mickey.

The darkness of the night was upon them now and she was happy to let it take her. It was all too much. I'm tired of fighting now. I'm ready. She closed her eyes and let the blackness envelope her, as she slipped into blissful unconsciousness. The last thing she saw was a green smile, sneering at her through the darkness.

Amongst the blurs of paramedics and bright lights, all Marie could recall was the agonising abdominal pain overwhelming her, making her feel as if she were being torn in two. Then there was just darkness, a sleep deeper than any she had ever experienced. For a moment she thought she might be dead. That this impenetrable blackness was all that was left for her now. But slowly she began to hear sounds through the void. A steady beep, gaining in volume, pulling her towards waking. She slowly opened her eyes, blinking hard against the bright white light suddenly surrounding her. Slowly, shapes began to form, blurred and strained, but solid and real nonetheless, coming into focus gradually until she began to grasp what they were.

The beeping was coming from the green glow of a heart monitor to her left, the jagged little lines making their way up and down and across the screen. It was both alien and comforting to her at the same time. Proof that she was alive. Behind it, she could see a silver foil balloon with 'Get well soon' in bright multicoloured lettering across its belly, dancing slightly to the air conditioner's tune. There were a few cards, with similar well wishes on the front and one with a little blue bear with a patch over its eye. She turned her head slowly and with great effort, taking in the rest of the room. A green fabric curtain half closed, white clinical walls, a print of Van Gogh's 'Almond Tree' in a thick black frame hanging on the wall. It was only then she realised he was there, to the right of her bed, awkwardly positioned on an uncomfortable-looking, blue plastic chair. There was a green woollen blanket half over him, and his head was resting on the back, causing it to sit at an odd angle. His eyes were closed, his mouth was slightly open, and from the rhythm of his breathing she could tell he was asleep. His collar was undone and he looked pale and worn. She followed his arm, the shirt sleeve hastily and half-heartedly rolled to the elbow, to his hand resting on the edge of the bed, the tips of his fingers against hers. She just watched him for a few moments, his chest rising and falling, still detached slightly from her surroundings. Everything still felt so fuzzy and she wondered if she was dreaming. Perhaps this was a trick of the dark hollow sleep she inhabited, there to give her false hope. But the longer she watched him, the clearer her thoughts became, as if a veil was lifting. She'd been sick, she remembered that, and then the pain. That awful pain burning through her. She suddenly wanted to touch him, to make sure he was real, to make sure she was indeed alive and awake. She moved her hand onto his, using all of her strength to squeeze his fingers.

He woke with a start, looking around him wildly for a short moment, as if seeking out an unknown threat, before his eyes rested on hers. His features crumpled with relief, and half crying half laughing, he embraced her, kissing her forehead and squeezing her hand in return. They remained there for a long time. She felt his warmth against her body and breathing him in, she knew it was real, and she felt happiness and relief wash over her.

"I thought I'd lost you."

"What happened?"

She felt him stiffen, ever so slightly the moment she asked the question. It was a reaction so small, so imperceptible, only she would notice it.

"Let's just concentrate on you getting well."

"What is it?"

"You're alive, that's all that matters."

She moved her head away from him and placed her hand on the side of his face. He stared at her, eyes welling with tears. She almost didn't want an answer now, but it was too late for that, they both knew it. "Please Malcolm, tell me what's wrong. Whatever it is, we can face it, together. What happened to me?"

"Maybe I should get the doctor."

"No, I want you to tell me. Please?"

He closed his eyes, and sighed heavily. A resigned sigh full of melancholy. "You were pregnant, but the baby, it was growing outside of the womb, it was inside your cervix. It ruptured and caused massive internal bleeding..."

She could feel everything spinning.

"In fact, you died sweetie. For almost a minute and a half, you were gone..."

She began to feel her stomach churning, and felt a pounding in her head.

"I thought I'd lost you, in the back of that ambulance, but they saved you. They brought you back to me. They had to take you into surgery..." He paused. Somehow that pause was scarier than anything else he said. What he held back, what he found the hardest to say would surely be the worst.

The pounding was louder, the nausea increasing, the room spinning faster and faster around them, as if Malcolm and she were the only two stationary objects. "They had to do it, to save you. It was the only way. I'm, I'm so sorry." With each word he got quieter, he spoke more softly. What are you so reluctant to say? "I'm sorry." It was a whisper now, he kept repeating it to himself, almost inaudibly. The pounding however, was getting louder. The room just a blur around them. "The doctor's had to give you a hysterectomy. I'm sorry, I'm so so sorry but they had to, to save you. They had to."

The pounding in her head drowned him out. She could see he was talking, but all she could hear was her own heartbeat in perfect synch with the beeping of the monitor, louder and louder, faster and faster. She felt as if she was falling, the hospital room, and Malcolm, began to shrink before her as she fell away from them, back into that dark sleep. Back into the nothingness.

Chapter Twenty One
-Present Day

It was so dark Marie couldn't tell where she was. She was walking along a long, narrow corridor and she could feel the walls on either side with outstretched arms. They felt cold. Beneath her feet she could feel a warm liquid, and it was then she realised she no longer wore shoes. She wiggled her toes. The liquid, whatever it was, felt thick like syrup. She didn't know what to do, so she continued to walk forwards, hoping eventually some crack of light, some sign would show her the way out. It felt like she'd walked for hours when she hit something solid. Frantically, she grabbed at the wall ahead of her, feeling for something, anything.

It's a door! She desperately sought out the handle, and with all her strength, yanked it open. Light suddenly poured through, momentarily blinding her. She blinked away the spots of white and red, trying to focus on what was ahead. There was a large mirror, with an elaborate black gilded frame sitting alone in an empty, featureless room, the only other item present being a bare bulb flickering from the centre of the ceiling. She turned back towards the corridor and felt horror rising from the pit of her stomach as she realised that the thick, warm liquid which coated the floors, and now covered her feet, was blood. Deep red, almost gelatinous blood. It lay an inch deep, giving the narrow room a red tinge of light.

Turning to face the mirror, she walked towards her reflection leaving red footprints with each trepidatious step. She stared at herself, almost not recognising the girl who looked back. She looked the same, she wore the same ragged white night dress, now stained red at the edges, she had the same dark circles under her eyes and bitten down nails. Except, Marie knew it wasn't her. Somehow, she knew the reflection was an imposter. An image of what she thought should be reflected there, rather than what actually was. Slowly, as if the imposter shared her thoughts, the edges of its lips began to curl up into a wicked smile, and its eyes narrowed, before it revealed a toothy, almost manic grin. The flesh began to rot away from its jaw, falling to the floor in blackened, shrivelled curls, until the entire bottom half of its skull was exposed. The bone and teeth seemed so white alongside the raw exposed flesh, until it began to glow an eerie green, getting brighter and brighter in the darkness.

Fear began to overwhelm her as she stared at this horrifying version of herself, aging and rotting before her eyes. She panicked and began to punch at the glass with closed fists, wanting so desperately to destroy the image, to escape from this monster. She hit the mirror hard enough to make cracks spiderweb outwards. The exposed edges of the glass sliced into her hand, adding to the blood that now seeped through the doorway into the tiny room. She didn't care that it hurt, hitting it again and again, as the blood began to rise past her ankles and the other Marie just continued to smile. Another hit, another crack, until the mirror shuddered and shook. The blood was almost at her knees now, rising faster and faster. But all she could think of, all she wanted was to destroy the image. Suddenly the glass exploded, sending tiny diamond-like pieces of glass around the room, which oozed and sank into the red sea rising around her. She covered her face, afraid the glass would blind her.

She stayed there a moment, her arms around her head, before slowly opening her eyes. Her heart sank. The mirror was gone, yes, the reflection destroyed, but there she was anyway, this other her, rotting and decaying but continuing to smile that green smile. It stood there staring and smiling as the blood suddenly vanished and the door, her only exit, slammed behind her. She stood transfixed, unsure where to go or what to do. Suddenly the other her opened its mouth wide and screeched a piercing cry, its jaw almost dislocating from its skull. It ran at her arms outstretched, the green grimace closing in.

Just as it reached her, just as its fingers closed around her throat, Marie awoke with a start. Her heart was pounding hard in her chest, and it took a moment for her to realise it had been a nightmare. She lay there, breathing heavily, looking wildly around as her eyes began to focus on her surroundings, searching for any unknown danger.

She was lying on a cold, concrete floor. The room was dark. The only light available was from the emergency exit sign above a nearby door, casting a green aura around the room. She could hear it humming. Her head was pounding, and her body ached. She felt incredibly thirsty, and wondered how long she had been unconscious. With great effort, her hands tied together in front of her with cable, she sat up and searched for some indication of time; a clock, a window, anything that would tell her how long she'd been there. How long she had been missing. The room appeared to be some kind of store room. It had bare breezeblock walls with scaffolding poles and rolls of wire fencing stacked in one corner, a group of empty plastic crates in another. The only window was small and narrow up towards the bare concrete ceiling. It had been painted with some kind of dark grey paint and no light was getting through. The position of the window made her think she might be in a basement. It was damp, the only other sound apart from the hum of the light being a dripping of water nearby. There was a set of metal shelves on one side, with what looked like old paint cans and various other items strewn across them. This room was a forgotten room, rarely thought about and even more rarely visited. Her heart sank at the thought. Please, don't let me be forgotten too.

She forced herself onto her feet, and limped towards the exit. Pushing on the handle hard, she heard the creak of the metal but the door remain closed tight against her body. Confused, she tried again, this time pushing even harder, but it was no use. The door didn't budge. It was then she noticed its rough soldered edge. She felt along its edges to confirm what she already knew. It's welded shut!

Frantically, she looked around her for another

way out. The window. She ran toward the wall which housed the little window and jumped, her bound hands clawing at the brick walls, desperately trying to reach it. But it was too high up. She searched out the crates, and using two as steps, she managed to reach it, pushing at it with all her strength, but it wouldn't budge. It appeared to be as permanently shut as the fire exit. She could break it, but even then she would never be able to fit through its narrow gap. She scraped away some of the paint, but she could see nothing beyond but darkness.

It was then she noticed the other door, hidden by the metal shelving unit, up a small flight of stairs. That's how I got down here. It was the only way in or out of the room. Scrambling off the crates, she pounded up the stairs and turned the handle. It was locked. She placed her ear against the cold wood. She could hear muffled sounds, some kind of music or perhaps talking, and she knew her kidnappers were on the other side.

She stumbled down the stairs and frantically checked every corner of the room. She felt every wall, checked behind every item, searching for a makeshift weapon, for any other way out. She felt like an insect, trapped inside a jar, bumping and buzzing up against the glass. There was nothing.

She slid against the wall and sat weeping on the cold, hard ground. She'd never felt more helpless. She reached into her pocket and retrieved a handkerchief. Before she wiped the tears and blood, she stopped, staring at the small white square of fabric in her hand, a little black 'M' embroidered in one corner. Mickey. The surge of grief hit her like a physical force, leaving her struggling to breathe, to cry out the pain she felt, an emotional pain which stung worse than anything physical she'd ever experienced, even the terrible day that ended her dreams of becoming a mother. She lay there for what felt like an eternity, her tears continuing to flow, stinging her eyes before tracking clean lines through her blackened, bloodied face, now contorted.

He was dead. Mickey was dead. And soon, she would be too.

Chapter Twenty Two
-Four Years Ago

Everything had become one long, unending dream state. She flitted in and out of sleep, always restless and drug induced, before waking to the blurry hospital room. But even when she was awake, she felt trapped inside a dream, as if nothing she saw or heard was real. There were doctors and specialists and nurses, all of them like aliens in this estranged clinical world. They used cold medical terms like 'intra-abdominal haemorrhage' and 'cervical ectopic pregnancy' which stung her when spoken, like some kind of barbaric, foreign language.

Malcolm never left her side. He remained steadfast, guarding her like a lone soldier, determined to keep going long after the war has been lost. He tried to be positive, to keep her spirits up, but she could see the devastation in his eyes. They would never have children. She would never know the butterfly kicks of her unborn baby, or smell the crook of its neck while it slept in her arms. When she thought about it, her stitches ached, as if her emotional pain was physical and real. She barely spoke, and ate and drank so little they decided to keep her on a drip. She measured time by the drop of that clear fluid. It was apparent how desperate Malcolm was to make it all better, to wave a wand or say some incantation that would fix everything by magic, but none existed. This was the reality and they had to face it.

But Marie felt the loss doubly hard. Everyone claimed they understood, after all, having a baby meant so much more for the woman than the man. She was the one biologically and physiologically built for the purpose of reproduction. It was supposed to be a woman's destiny, her reason for being. But that wasn't it, not completely. It was because Marie not only mourned the loss of an imagined child, she mourned the loss of Malcolm too. He would want to stay, to marry her anyway, that wasn't the problem. He was a gentleman, a man of honour, a man of loyalty, who believed a handshake was a legal contract and a man's word was all he had. No, he would never leave her, but she couldn't stay. She knew how important having a child and heir was to him. She couldn't be the reason he lost the chance for something so precious. It was the right thing to do, no matter how painful it would be.

And so, she slept and mourned, mourned and slept, waiting for the strength to say goodbye to everything she loved.

"What about this one, is this like it?"

He'd brought her bridal magazines in an attempt to take her mind off the pains of the present, to look ahead to future joys, but it made everything worse. He was playing a game now, trying to guess what her dress looked like, selecting those amongst the pages which he believed best reflected her personality. He started to make a joke of it, clearly choosing the tackiest dresses he could find, anything to make her smile. On this occasion he pointed at a particularly heinous meringue of a dress, all chiffon and diamantes. "That seems very you! We could get you a tiara to go with it."

He smiled that charming smile that drew her in the first night they met, but she could see sorrow behind it. She wouldn't budge, remaining steadfast and determined in her state of self-pity. She didn't think anything could make her smile ever again. He seemed to read her mind again, the way he had on so many occasions. She usually treasured his telepathic ability, comforted by the fact he knew her so well, but she hated him for it right now. Now more than ever, she wanted to keep her thoughts to herself. They were too personal, too heart-breaking to share, even with him.

"Look, I know everything seems terrible right now, like nothing will ever be good again. But we'll get through this, together. You will smile again, we both will. We'll laugh and grow past this, maybe it will even bring us closer together, make us stronger. It will be ok, I promise you. And after the wedding..."

"There won't be a wedding."

He looked utterly shocked, dumbfounded by an imaginary blow. "I don't understand."

The tears began to pour the moment she began to speak. She thought they were all used up, that she had no more left to shed. She saw the drip in her mind's eye, with each single droplet entering her veins, then working their way to her eyes where they immediately fell again as tears. "I love you Malcolm, I do, with all my heart. And that's why I can't stay, because you deserve a family, you deserve someone who can give you what you want, what you've always wanted. And... I can't. I can't."

He reached for her, and held her, her head nuzzled in his chest, wetting his shirt with tears. He just sat there, holding her, swaying slightly, as one might with a child, letting her cry herself out, just as he had so many times these past few days. She wanted to push him away, to remain strong and determined, but the truth was she needed his arms around her, she needed to be held and comforted. Lately, it was the only thing that helped, the only thing that made the pain bearable.

When her wailing gradually quieted, and her breathing slowed to just a sniff, he moved her head from her chest and cupped her face with both hands, one on either side, each thumb wiping away the tears. "You listen to me, Marie, and you listen good. I love you. I love you more than anything on this earth. I won't insult you by pretending I'm not devastated by this, of course I am. Yes, I wanted children, we both did, but life doesn't care about the plans you've made. This is the way it is now, and yes it's sad, but I know we can get through this. I know, together, we can get through anything. I see what you're trying to do, and why you think it's right, but it's not going to happen. Because, I need you, and nothing would make me be without you. Nothing."

"But I can't have children." The words stabbed at her chest like a knife – it was the first time she said them aloud.

"I don't care, I love you."

"You don't have to stay, anyone would understand."

"I don't care, I love you."

"But you're giving up so much."

"But I'm getting you!"

"Malcolm..."

"Marie, look at me...I don't care. Whatever you say, I don't care. I love you, and I'm going to marry you and spend the rest of our lives showing you just how much you mean to me. There is nothing you can say that would drive me away from you. You're the other half of me, I can't exist without you."

He smiled at her now, and this time it wasn't forced. It was genuine and filled with love, and she knew she would never leave him. She couldn't. She believed him. They would be ok. Together they were invincible, they could face any challenge life threw up. Apart, they would wither and die.

Chapter Twenty Three
-Present Day

His headache was fast becoming a migraine, and the pills he forced down with a slug of tepid vending machine coffee did little to help. It was only worsened by the flashbacks he kept having. His brain refused to concentrate on the here and now, instead veering back to that same horrible moment, that rejected kiss in the rain, repeating over and over in his mind like a broken record. The kiss that ended any illusions about being with Marie, of the hero saving the damsel in distress and riding off into the sunset.

He threw his mug in frustration, the white china detonating as it hit the wall. He stared at the carnage a moment, thinking about how it looked a bit like a crime scene. The mug was the body, now broken and empty, and the coffee was the blood, which spread and stained everything it touched. He smirked to himself at the thought.

The door to his tiny office suddenly flew open. Detective Mark Haywood stood in the doorway, a look of concern across his red, sweaty face. Mark was a stout man, with terrible dress sense and an even worse comb over. His stomach always peeked out between the buttons of his grubby shirts, threatening to make a break for freedom at any moment, and he always had his mouth open, which made him appear utterly gormless. Fraser hated him. Not because of his bad hygiene or profuse sweating, and not because he was a bad police officer (he had, in point of fact, been very good in his youth, having been awarded several commendations). He hated him because he was lazy. He expelled more energy trying to avoid work than he would if he actually just did his job. After eighteen years on the force, he'd lost all enthusiasm or interest, and every form he submitted and case he worked on made that painfully apparent.

"What do you want Haywood?"

"I wanted to check you were ok, I thought I heard something." His beady eyes moved towards the splinters of china and the brown liquid now staining the carpet, before flitting back to Fraser.

"I dropped my mug that's all."

"You dropped it?"

"That's what I said."

It was apparent Detective Haywood didn't believe him, but it was also apparent that he didn't care enough to probe further. Maybe his laziness had its uses after all. "Okay, just checking...Oh, the enquiry office rang up, there's a man in for you."

"Who is it?"

"Hmmm, can't remember. That's funny, isn't it? I only heard it a few minutes ago."

"That is funny, Haywood. It's hilarious." Either Mark didn't notice the blatantly sarcastic tone, or he was ignoring it. Fraser didn't really care either way. "Did this mystery man say what he wanted?"

"Hmmm, yes. Something about his wife going missing. Marie something or other."

Fraser felt every muscle in his body tense when he heard her name. "Missing? What do you mean missing?"

"Yes, he said it's part of a case you're dealing with. I told the Enquiry assistant we don't deal with missing persons but apparently the man was quite insistent. Malcolm, that's his name. Knew I would get there in the end."

As Mark walked away chuckling to himself, the door slowly closed behind him, causing the room to darken as it did. Fraser sat there, frozen for a moment, unable to process what he had just been told. Why would Malcolm come to him? He was investigating him, he had interrogated him twice since taking his case and it was made abundantly clear by both parties that neither could stand the sight of the other. And what about Marie? What happened to her? Malcolm would have to be pretty desperate to come here for help.

For a moment, he entertained the idea that Marie left Malcolm for him. That she changed her mind and realised what a monster Malcolm really was. That his kiss, his desperate plea, had worked. But deep down, he knew that wasn't true.

The lift to the enquiry office seemed painfully slow. He watched the illuminated numbers as he passed each floor, a countdown to something terrible. He had to pass the security monitors before entering the public side, and a quick glimpse showed Malcolm pacing back and forth, his features distorted in a look of fear. That brief image was more than enough to make him realise Marie was in danger.

"Let's step inside an interview room." He ushered Malcolm through another secure door, only just remembering to move the sign to 'In Use'.

"Marie is missing. So are my men, and the car. He has them."

"Calm down, maybe she's just taken a detour or went to a friend's."

"No. My men call in every thirty minutes to let me know everything's okay, and I haven't heard from them in four hours. Their phones are switched off, so is Marie's. She was meeting me for dinner and she never showed. I know my wife, Detective."

"Maybe you don't know her as well as you think..."

Malcolm seemed to snap, losing control the second the words left Fraser's mouth. He grabbed him by the shirt and forced him against the wall. Their faces were mere millimetres apart, so close Fraser could feel his shallow breaths as Malcolm spat every word he spoke. "Do you think for one second I don't know you're in love with my wife? Do you honestly believe I was unaware of your little meetings? Your little secret messages and calls? I tolerated you because I knew she was having a difficult time, and it seemed to help her deal with everything. Her happiness is paramount, so I put up with your pathetic little crush all these months."

He released Fraser, who stood panting a moment, wrestling with a million thoughts and feelings. Malcolm had known everything.

"We don't have time for this. We need to find her. You know what Savage is capable of. We don't have a lot of time."

Dozens of crime scene photographs began to flash through Fraser's mind. A slide show of blood and bone. He tried to form his thoughts properly, to push aside all of the shame and heartbreak and focus on finding her. He began to check through each case involving Savage and his crew, focusing particularly on the female victims. They were usually kept alive for approximately twenty-four hours. During that period, they were taken to an unknown location, tortured, sometimes raped, and eventually murdered. Fraser shuddered at the thought, Marie's face now transposed on the bodies he'd seen. Her eyes now frozen in horror. He shook himself out of it. He was no use to her letting emotion get the better of him.

"Okay, tell me everything you know. Where and when had they last checked in?"

"Four hours ago, at the park where you kissed her."

Fraser was stunned, the realisation that they had never truly been alone, that Malcolm had his goons watching them the entire time. They just stared at each other a moment. Both were filled with a deep-seeded hatred for the other, but both loved Marie enough for concern to override that hate. Bravado would have to wait.

"Okay, if they check in every half an hour, that means she went missing between eight and eight thirty. Give me the reg of the car they were in. I'll check the traffic cameras, and track it from the park." Pre-empting the question, Malcolm handed him a scribbled note containing the details of the car, the men, their mobile phones and descriptions, everything. "For me to check this, I'll have to file a formal missing person report."

"Do what you have to do. But mark my words Detective, when I find Savage, and I will, there will be no police involvement or official reports."

The words hung heavy in the air between them, an understanding forming. They would form a shaky alliance built precariously out of the love they both held in common and the fear of losing her, but when the time came, when they were at the last stand with Savage, they would revert back to being enemies once again. There was no other way.

As Fraser ran to his Sergeant's office, taking two stairs at a time, clutching the ragged piece of paper in his clammy hand, he thought back to his childhood. Of play battles between the cops and robbers, between the 'good guys' and 'bad guys'. In all those games, throughout his entire career, those two forces had never colluded before. He had never walked through the grey gulf between them, always seeing things as black and white, us and them. The entire notion filled him with trepidation.

But then he thought of Marie. He pictured her alone and terrified, crying in the dark, and as he knocked on his boss's door he wondered to himself – just how far would he go for love?

Chapter Twenty Four

It'd been a difficult few months. When she left the hospital that day, the world outside suddenly seemed so vast and overwhelming. She immediately wanted to retreat back to her hospital bed, safe and warm, with the beeps of the heart monitor constantly reminding her she was alright, she was alive. The cold air bit at her pallid cheeks, and the stitches in her abdomen ached with every step, every twinge a reminder of what she lost, of the part of her that was missing.

Recovery was difficult and took its toll both mentally and physically. The hospital insisted she see a grief counsellor, but one look at the photographs of two smiling, red headed children on his desk and she'd been put off ever returning. Instead, she relied on Malcolm and Sara, both offering themselves to her as nurse and counsel.

Malcolm took time off from his work, putting his deputy Richard in charge, whose wife Linda came over often to clean the house and cook their meals, offering her very practical form of therapy to Marie. All in all, she was lucky, she knew that. But, no matter how much time passed or how many self-help books she read, no matter how she distracted herself with reorganising the wedding after its postponement or what reassuring thing she told herself, she felt hollow. Physically and emotionally hollow.

The medication helped, Prozac and tea fast becoming her favourite breakfast, and eventually a chat room at a website for infertile women offered a much needed sounding board, a kinship with women who truly understood her pain. In time, slowly, she began to smile again, to look forward. The burden of loss lessened little by little, creating room for new things, for positive things in her life.

Malcolm had been her rock throughout, and now that Sara was leaving, unable to postpone her new life abroad any longer, she relied on him more than ever. Every day he showed her, in small, seemingly insignificant gestures, just how much she meant to him. On so many occasions, she felt guilt biting at her heels, trying to drag her back to depression, but he steadied her and held her hand as they moved closer with every passing day.

With time, she would stop resenting the young mothers she saw out with their prams, or secretly hating the glowing women with their large swollen bellies who seemed to have increased in number dramatically since the operation (or perhaps she only noticed them more than before). In the meantime, she was alright. She had survived, and life would go on for her. For both of them.

"I have something for you."

She looked up from her book to find him standing there with a large navy blue envelope in one hand and a champagne glass in the other. He was wearing a grey pin stripe suit with crisp edges and a pale pink pocket square. He had no tie on, and his top collar button was undone just enough for you to see the dark shadow of hair peeking out. He looked incredibly attractive, which made Marie a little disappointed he would be leaving shortly. After multiple medical appointments, and countless gynecological checks, she had only just begun to feel the twinges of arousal again that used to always accompany the sight of her husband in a good suit, or the smell of cedar wood on the pillow next to her. I wish he never had to go back to work.

After taking so much time off for her, the first taken since he'd begun work as a teenager, after being so supportive and understanding, she could hardly be mad at him for going back now. After all, even she was starting to get stir crazy stuck inside after all this time. "Rest, rest," was the constant mantra of everyone around her, but she was beginning to heal, both outside and in. Her scars were now a pink colour, instead of the angry red smile that had been there before, fading over time along with her grief. For the first time since her hospitalisation, she wanted to get out and do things again, and so the orders and encouragement for continued quiet and relaxation, however well intentioned, were beginning to cause resentment.

"What's that?"

"Open it and see."

The envelope was thick and expensive feeling, and smelled vaguely of vanilla. Inside was a card from the Cliftonwood spa in nearby Berkshire. It was a place she had fond memories of, having spent a very romantic weekend there with Malcolm not long after they began dating. The building itself was a stunning 17th century manor house, surrounded by hundreds of acres of National Trust forest and decorative gardens. She remembered how, wandering through the grounds, she felt like Elizabeth Bennett exploring the home of her true love, Mr. Darcy. It had been blissful. She smiled at the memory.

"I thought Sara and you could have a girls' weekend before she leaves next week. I've arranged everything – massages, manicures, champagne brunches, the works. What do you think?"

"Can you not come with us?" She knew the answer to the question before it left her lips, but felt the need to ask it anyway, just in case.

"I'm sorry baby, I have a very important business meeting this weekend. There's been an issue with one of my associates and if I don't get it sorted out, there could be serious consequences for other deals. I wish I could, I really do."

He leaned in and kissed her forehead. Ever since the hospital, it had become his gesture of reassurance. His way of saying, "I love you." without saying anything at all.

"I understand. It was worth a try."

"I think it will be good for you to have a change of location. Plus, it's a great opportunity for you and Sara to spend some real time together before she leaves."

The thought of Sara leaving made her heart hurt, but she knew she was going on an adventure with the man she loved, and if she was in her position, she would be doing exactly the same thing. "Sounds wonderful. Thank you."

Upon arrival at the spa, they headed straight to the bar on Sara's insistence, ordering cocktail after cocktail. It felt like the old days again, when they would go to bars during 'Happy Hour' and order as many half price drinks as they could before they became unaffordable again. Those evenings had always ended the same way, drunk by nine o'clock and eating a greasy pizza on the way home, Sara carrying her high heels and Marie, slightly nauseous, trying to steer them both home. The setting was definitely classier, and they'd both moved on and grown, but being around her remained as easy and fun as it had always been. Marie would miss her dearly.

"Charlie was having a kind of leaving to do with his friends last weekend, and he got so drunk he ended up sleeping in the wrong room. He woke up spooning his friend Rick's fifty-five-year-old mother. It's a good thing I'm not the jealous type, huh?"

They both laughed unapologetically loudly, Sara getting to the point during her stories where she was unable to actually speak, tears of laughter filling her eyes, holding her side as if she might actually split in two from laughing so hard. It was the happiest Marie had felt since before everything happened. This realisation brought back the memories she'd temporarily clouded with alcohol and jokes, and she began to laugh a little less, staring at her now empty glass. Sara noticed it immediately.

"How are you coping, Marie?"

"I'm getting there."

"You seem better. It's good to hear that squeaky, high pitched laugh of yours again."

She smiled. "Its feels pretty good to be laughing again."

"I'm really gonna miss you, you know that right? But this won't be the end of everything. There's Skype and email, and I expect you to visit as often as possible. I mean, what's the point of marrying a rich man if you can't spend his money on holiday after holiday? Oh, and on treating your favourite cousin to expensive meals when you visit her of course."

They both laughed, but they were tinged with a sadness at the knowledge that this weekend marked the end of an era. Yes, they would always be in contact, yes she would visit, but they both knew things were changing, and they would never be the same again.

"I love you, Sara. I really do. Thank you, for everything."

"God, don't get all soppy on me, you'll make me cry. I think we definitely need another drink, don't you?"

"Definitely."

"Garcon, another round for my gorgeous cousin and I, and don't skimp on the vodka!" Sara's phone began to vibrate, moving slowly towards the edge of the bar, as if it was trying to make a break for it. "Oh, it's Charlie. He must be missing me already, bless. Hey baby, you already suicidal without me?" She had a broad smile, but when Marie heard the muffled sound of a voice on the other side of the phone, it quickly dropped, replaced by a look of confused concern. "What? Is she ok? Okay, which hospital? I'm on my way. I know, I know but she'll be fine. I'll be home as soon as I can. I love you too, bye bye." She hung up, raising from the bar just as their icy red cocktails arrived in front of them. "Charlie's mum had a heart attack. I'm so sorry hun, but I'm gonna have to go back to London."

"Oh my God, that's awful. Is she okay?"

"Oh she's fine, the only thing that'll kill that witch is if a little girl in pig tails with ruby slippers threw a bucket of water at her."

"Sara! That's terrible..." Marie was trying to feign outrage, but she was smirking as she said it. She'd been regaled with story after story about her 'Monster in-law' and the many ways she tried to keep Charlie her little boy. Every time she made a passive aggressive remark about Sara's haircut or weight, or cried when she didn't get her own way about their wedding plans, Sara began to resent her more and more. The breaking point came the day she had a 'panic attack' and needed Charlie to be by her side, which just so happened to be the day they were meant to be going to Scotland for a romantic weekend (an engagement present from his musician friends). Sara had snapped and called her 'Mrs. Bates'. A blazing row followed, with the future mother-in-law telling Sara she wasn't good enough 'for her baby boy' and Sara retorting that she was a 'fat, ugly cow who needed to get laid', resulting in a mutual agreement to spend as little time with each other as possible. Sara hadn't seen her since.

"I'm so sorry Marie, I really wanted to spend time with you before I left."

"Don't be silly! I think a heart attack is a pretty good excuse to bail. I'm just sorry she's sick."

"Don't be, the bitch probably timed this deliberately so we wouldn't go on Wednesday."

They both smirked at each other, the kind of smirk that says, 'That shouldn't be funny, but it is.' Sara grabbed her bag and went to get up, before lifting the cocktail and gulping it down. "For the road. I have a feeling I'll need it."

"I'll grab our bags."

"No, you should stay and enjoy yourself. Don't leave on my account."

"No, don't be silly. I'm not gonna make you go back to London alone. Besides, it wouldn't be the same without you."

"Are you sure? I hate the idea of ruining your weekend!"

"You haven't ruined anything, these few hours have been exactly what I needed. And Malcolm said he is working from home this weekend, so I won't be alone. I'll surprise him with takeout and a bottle of wine!"

Sara grabbed Marie, pulling her in for a long hug, and they stayed there a moment, both knowing that this was the end of an era.

By the time Marie made it home, the street lights hummed and most of London slept. She was tired, the buzz of the alcohol having slowly transformed into a dull, drowsy headache. She longed for her bed.

As Mickey parked the car, she stared at her own reflection in the dull shine of the lift walls and thought about Sara, about losing her to someone else, to another land. She wanted to be happy for her, but her sense of loss overwhelmed any of the joy, leaving her feeling deflated.

Exiting the lift, she entered the large private hallway, its bare concrete walls giving it a sombre tone. The building was a converted factory, and they had the entire top floor to themselves. The property developers had been sensitive to the listed building, maintaining its industrial roots in the bare brick walls, wrought iron staircases and large panelled windows. Often, Marie liked to imagine what it would have looked like back in the day, busy with weavers and workers. Sometimes, in moments like this, when she heard her footsteps echoing as she walked toward their front door, the building felt like a big, empty creature, lonely and sad now that everyone was gone, longing for the days when it was so full of life. For the first time, she realised she had something in common with it.

When she got inside, she could hear muffled voices in the next room and saw the thin line of light shining from beneath the door into the living area. She was surprised that Malcolm was up at this late hour, and even more so at the fact that he had company. As she approached the large heavy door, she began to pick out multiple voices, all of which sounded barbed and angry. She wondered what exactly it was she was about to interrupt. The voices, getting louder and angrier as she approached, definitely weren't the sounds of a sombre business meeting or a jovial social gathering.

As she pushed the door open, the light now

escaping the room within, she could discern specific words coming from the kitchen beyond the living area. It was separated from her by half a partition wall which obscured their origins, but allowed her to hear what was going on beyond.

"Don't fucking lie, Dee. We know it was you..." She recognised the voice immediately as Richard, Malcolm's long-time friend and business associate. He spat the words out, the hatred made clear with each syllable. "...Just tell us where it is Dee, and this can stop."

"I swear on my Mother's grave, I had nothing to do with this. You have to believe me. You know I wouldn't do that to you, you know that, please...please stop."

This voice, which she assumed belonged to this 'Dee' person, was so filled with fear and desperation that hearing him plead as he did made the hair on the back of her neck stand on end. She'd never heard another human being sound so terrified before, and it made her fear what she would find.

"Bullshit Dee." There was a loud bang, a cry in pain.

She began to imagine the worst case scenarios, that something awful had happened to Malcolm, that he'd been hurt, or worse, killed.

"Tell us!"

"Please, I don't know..."

Another bang, another cry in pain, the sound of someone crying.

"David..."

Marie stopped suddenly, her heart now pounding loudly in her ears. This voice was a voice she knew better than her own. This calm, even voice amongst the anger and terror. This was the voice of her fiancé. This voice belonged to Malcolm.

"...Do you think I enjoy seeing you like this? This breaks my heart, it truly does. I have considered you a loyal employee, an ally, a friend even, for all these years, and you go and do this to me? I would give anything to change this situation we find ourselves in, but you knew there would be consequences to your actions David. You knew what would happen and you did it anyway. You only have yourself to blame."

"Please Mr. Carter..."

"Don't say another word about not knowing. Do you think I would do something like this if I wasn't one hundred percent sure? If I hadn't checked and double checked? Everyone here knows it was you David, so don't insult my intelligence."

They were silent a moment, as if the words which had just been spoken were hanging heavy in the air, and that those involved were letting them sink in and be made solid.

"I... I'm sorry. I'll tell you everything, please."

It was spoken so quietly, Marie had to strain to hear it over the pounding of her heartbeat inside her own head. She was afraid. Afraid that what she was about to see would change her life forever, but she had to see, it was too late to go back.

It took a moment for the scene before her to sink in. There, in the centre of their kitchen, was a man, bloodied and beaten, tied to a chair, his wrists and ankles wrapped with bloodstained rope. Marie had never seen him before, although it was difficult to tell, his face was so swollen and bloodied that one of his eyes had almost shut completely. The chair to which he was tethered stood on a large, clear plastic sheet, secured to the hard wood floors with duct tape, and so spattered with drops of vivid red, it resembled a Jackson Pollock painting.

Richard stood to the left, rubbing his knuckles, presumably readying himself for round two. There were two other men behind the chair, leaning against the kitchen cabinets. She recognised them from Capone's, both having regularly tended the door. Malcolm stood at the front of the chair, his back to her. He seemed to be staring at the figure in the centre of all of this, daring him to repeat his denials.

As she entered their view, one of the men at the back nudged the other and nodded in her direction as they both stepped forwards. Richard was the first to say something, dropping his hands to his sides as if in some futile attempt to hide what was clearly going on, or at least, his part in it. "Marie..."

Malcolm spun around, and as his eyes met hers, she saw shock and panic. For a few seconds, they all stood there in silence, rooted to the spot, all afraid to speak or move. Every one of them unsure what to do next.

The man in the chair raised his head, with obvious difficulty, the whites of his eyes a stark contrast to the dark maroon of its surroundings. As he spoke, the words almost bubbled with the blood and spit in his mouth, and his eyes reached out to her, they begged her, to save him. "Miss, please help me, please..."

"Quiet." Richard spat the words at the man and raised his hand in a threat as one would to a disobedient dog. The man flinched, but continued to stare at her, pleading with her. It was all too much, every instinct in her told her to run. So that's what she did; she ran.

She ran towards the front door, Malcolm following close behind, yelling her name, begging her to stop. He caught up with her just as she reached her hand towards the handle, grabbing her arm, and spinning her around to face him.

"Marie, please don't go, let me explain."

"Explain? Explain what Malcolm? How could there ever be an explanation for that."

"Please Marie, you know me, you know I would never hurt you. Please just stay a moment and let me explain everything to you. After that, if you want to go, and never see me again, I won't stop you. I won't go after you. You'll never see me again. Please, just give me the chance to explain, please?"

She felt torn in two. Surely, after what she had just witnessed, escaping, calling the Police was the only thing she could do. But the other half of her wanted to hear him explain this away, so she could still be with him. The other part of her loved him too much to go.

"Marie?"

Hearing him say her name like that, his voice full of such desperation, she knew she had to hear him out. "Ok, explain."

"Let's go into the office for some privacy."

They walked into the office, her eyes just beginning to adjust to the darkness of the room, just beginning to make out the shapes of objects, when he switched on the antique brass desk lamp. It wasn't bright enough to illuminate the whole room, and cast long, sinister shadows around them both. She shivered involuntarily. He pulled the large leather chair toward her, but she declined. She wanted to stand, to look him in the eye. For what seemed like an age, he said nothing, collecting his thoughts, forming his words. Please say something. Please make this better.

"I don't know where to start... What I do, for a living, how I make my money, it isn't how you think. I am the head of a group of individuals which operates throughout the city in a number of businesses, some legitimate, some not legitimate."

"Not legitimate? You're in there beating the living shit out of some guy!"

"That is an unfortunate incident, and a rare one. I'm sorry you had to see that. In my line of work, sometimes, sadly, violence is necessary."

"What are you saying?"

"I often work outside the confines of the law, that's the nature of my job."

"Would you just spit it out? Stop skirting around the edges of this and tell me. TELL ME!"

"I... I'm a criminal."

"What? I don't understand...you own the club, and those other bars. You rent properties, you trade in antiques and art. That's what you said, that's your work."

"And I do those things. I do own bars and clubs like Capone's, I do rent properties, I do deal in art. I never lied to you about those things."

"Then what are you talking about?"

"Those aren't my main role, they're more like by-products, places where the money I make elsewhere is filtered."

"Are you talking about money laundering?"

"Yes."

Marie was stunned. Every conversation they'd ever had, every word he said about work was flashing in her mind, a montage of lies and half-truths. She closed her eyes tight, trying to stop the images spinning in her head, the feeling of motion sickness rising in her stomach. She felt a hand on her arm, an attempt to comfort her, which would normally sooth her pain, but now felt like fire. "Don't touch me!"

She pulled her self away, moving to behind the desk, to the furthest point from him in the room. A spot where the shade would hide her grief while she gathered her thoughts. "You said you would be honest with me. You promised!"

"I never lied to you Marie, not once."

"An omitted truth is exactly the same as a blatantly told lie Malcolm. Don't you dare pretend otherwise!"

He paused a moment, tears rising in his eyes. "You're right. You're absolutely right. I should have told you, I wanted to, I swear. I wanted to more than anything else in the world. It's just, I was so afraid of losing you. I was being selfish. I should have told you."

"Then tell me now. None of this 'legitimate' or 'illegitimate' bullshit. No managerial speak or sugar coating. Be honest, like you promised."

"Ok...you deserve to know the truth. I do trade in antiques and art. That wasn't a lie. But the truth is, most of it is stolen. I have people who work for me, people who steal these things on my behalf. I also trade in high end stolen cars, and sometimes weapons. I have several brothels running, as well as illegal gambling establishments. I launder the money made from these things through properties and businesses I own, like Capone's and I blackmail or bribe local officials and Police to look the other way. I'm a criminal, as I said. But I'm not just any common criminal, I'm his boss. That's the truth. I'm not a good person, and I don't deserve someone like you. I know that. I just, I wanted to keep you as long as I could, so I hid you from that world. From my world, and I'm sorry for that. I truly am."

Marie felt as if the floor beneath her feet, the very foundations of her world, had been suddenly ripped away. She was falling now. Falling with no end in sight. "I don't...I don't know..."

"I'm sorry I'm not the man you thought I was, the one you deserve. But please believe me when I say I love you, with every part of my being, I love you."

Those words stung. Vinegar poured on open sores. "That man...you hurt people?" Marie wasn't sure if it was a question or a statement, but it was something she needed to know. They started down this rabbit hole, falling through the darkness, and the only way to reach the bottom was to hear everything, to know it all.

He paused, his bottom lip trembling, as if the words would not come. As if he couldn't bear to say them. "Yes. I hurt people."

"Have you killed people?"

He paused, his gaze suddenly shifting downwards.

"Malcolm...Have you killed?"

"Yes."

She crumpled to the floor, winded, deflated. She had reached the bottom of the rabbit hole, but there was no Wonderland. There was only blood and mud.

Chapter Twenty Five
-Present Day

How long had it been? Marie could only guess. Four hours? Five hours? However long it had been, it was too long, her fear never dissipating, her tears running dry. She managed to saw off the cable tie which bound her wrists together by using the sharp edge of a broken scaffolding pole, but her wrists still ached, the red, raw line visible even in the dull, green light.

No one had come, nothing had happened. She began to wonder if they intended to leave her there, to let her rot away. A slow death of starvation and dehydration trapped inside this concrete tomb with the rest of the forgotten things. In case they did return, she placed some loose bricks into a now dry and empty paint can. It wouldn't be the most effective weapon, but it was better than no weapon at all, and she would be damned if she was going down without a fight.

She kept seeing Mickey. Every time she closed her eyes, she saw his face, pale and clammy, his eyes glassy and dead. The image stabbed at her heart. He died trying to save her. He could have run, he could have played dead, but he didn't. He kept fighting, right until the end, and that's exactly what she would do. She thought about Malcolm. She pondered the choices she had made, the compromises, made in the name of love. Would she have made those same decisions if she knew how it would end? If she knew it would lead to this? Perhaps. All she knew for certain was that she had made them, they were what they were, and she had no one to blame but herself. And she thought about Fraser. She thought about his kindness and his honesty, and it broke her heart. Maybe, in another life, if she had met him at a bar instead of Malcolm, maybe everything would have played out differently. He was exactly the type of man she would have pictured herself with when she was younger, when she imagined her future husband. She could easily have filled the shoes of a Policeman's wife. But that wasn't her fate. The truth was, there was no time for regrets, especially now.

When the noise of bolts being shifted and keys being turned echoed through the room, Marie suddenly jolted back to the present. She moved quickly, hiding behind the scaffolding pipes, crouching in the shadows, makeshift weapon in hand.

She heard whispering, and the dull hollow thud of slow methodical footsteps down wooden steps. There were two of them, perhaps three. She angled her head towards the shaft of green light filtering through between two of the pipes, craning her neck to see them without them seeing her.

The first, a thin greasy man with a black tracksuit on and a sharp nose, was followed closely by a slightly overweight one, with too much gel on his mousey hair and a maroon red hooded sweatshirt.

The third man stood out of sight, obscured by the roll of wire fencing, only a blue baseball cap visible.

"Where the fuck is she?"

"Relax, Lee, it's not like she could go anywhere is it?"

"Did you see that ass though? Phew! I would destroy that."

All three of them laughed. Marie could feel her heart thumping inside her chest. She held her breath, convinced it was beating so hard, so fast, that they would surely hear it.

The thin, greasy one raised his hand to quiet the other two. "Oh…Little lady…come out, come out wherever you are." He sang the words, as if the situation they found themselves in was ordinary. As if it was just a simple game of hide and go seek. Marie began to feel sick, adrenaline and fear surging through her veins as she watched them splitting off from one another, seeking her out.

"We won't hurt you, we just wanna talk."

She lost sight of the baseball cap, as the larger one made his way toward her hiding place, stifling a laugh. She gripped the handle of the tin so hard, it cut into her hands. She could almost feel her heart pressing against the inside of her rib cage with every beat, with every step. Just a little closer.

As he neared the pipes, as he closed in on her, she could smell his sweat and cheap aftershave. It made her want to vomit. He saw her a moment too late, a paint tin suddenly hitting his jaw. The thud echoed around the concrete walls and blood burst from his face as his heavy frame dropped like a tree giving way to an axe swing.

She moved quickly, acutely aware that the other two would be heading straight for her. Leaping from her hiding place, she kicked the scaffolding pipe nearest her, sending them crashing down behind her. She didn't see the baseball cap, but heard a yelp and a thud over her shoulder. As she sprinted for the stairs, the greasy one lunged at her, causing them both to trip over the now scattered pipes and hit the floor. She landed hard on one of the pipes, winding her and sending shooting pain through her back, but the adrenaline coursing through her veins spurred her on. Her attacker lay to her right, moaning. She grabbed her paint can and forced herself up, gritting her teeth with the pain in her rib cage. She hit him, once, twice, three times, aiming for his face. He yelped and twitched with each blow until he was left gurgling and unconscious.

She knew the baseball cap would be on her any moment. She had to get through that door. She dragged herself up the stairs, limping now, the fall on the pipes leaving her right ankle swollen and sore. It took every ounce of strength she had to drag herself up each step, the mottled light through the open door acting as a beacon.

A figure appeared at the top of the staircase. He was just a shadow to her, tall and menacing, but instantly, in her heart she knew who he was. It only took a second for her to spot the silhouette of the gun in his hand, the outline sharp against the white light behind him. She froze in her tracks, still clinging to the handle of her weapon, her mind racing a million miles a second. Part of her thought about swinging, about going down fighting, but the survival instinct in her screamed to drop the tin, to live to fight another day. The shadow stood there, still apart from his hand gripping and re-gripping the gun at his side, as if waiting for her, daring her to try something. The survival instinct won the battle, and she released the handle, the tin falling down each of the steps with a metallic thud. She suddenly felt exhausted, as every bone in her body ached and cried out for sleep.

The fat male waddled to the bottom of the stairs, his hands clasping an oily rag to his bloody nose, his face growing whiter by the second. He was followed closely by an athletic looking black male, as he limped sheepishly into view, his baseball cap in his hands and his eyes lowered. The other man lay motionless, only a leg visible from where she stood. They both appeared to be as afraid of the dark figure as she was, like naughty children awaiting their punishment.

He began to descend slowly, taking each stair with deliberate, heavy steps. As he approached her, she began to discern his features. He was younger than she'd expected, perhaps mid to late twenties, and his head was shaved close on the side, but slightly longer on the top. He had a scar on his right cheek, which sat jagged and uneven on his pale skin, having clearly never received the stitches it should have. He wore a grey t-shirt and dark jeans, a chain hanging from one pocket. What she noticed most about him was his eyes. They were such a dark brown they were almost black in colour, the iris and the pupil blending into one another with no distinct edge. They were the eyes of a cold, unfeeling man, and they terrified her as they stared, never leaving hers as he got closer.

He stopped so he was standing on the same stair as she pressed herself against the wall behind her, her hand clutching the banister at the nape of her back. He stayed there a moment, just staring at her. She was transfixed, unable to scream, unable to move. He broke eye contact with her, and moved his eyes down to her feet, then slowly up towards her face again, as if he was studying every inch of her, invading her body with his eyes. When his eyes once again met hers, he slowly curled his mouth into a sneer which filled Marie with a deeper fear than she'd ever felt before.

Suddenly, he raised the hand holding the gun, and struck her hard across the face. She felt her cheek give way instantly under the force, and her mouth fill with blood as she plummeted down the steps, settling at the feet of the two goons. Her head felt like it was splitting in two and she was barely clutching to consciousness as she lay choking and sputtering. She heard the same slow, deliberate steps as he descended towards her. She didn't dare look, afraid that if she did he would strike her again.

"Tell me boys, how the fuck do three of my best and brightest get their asses handed to them by a girl?"

"She got the drop on us, boss."

"Give me one good reason why I shouldn't put you down like the mutts you are?"

"Oh please boss, we're sorry...it won't happen again."

"Yeah, we swear it won't."

He sighed deeply, making his annoyance and disgust obvious with each drawn out breath. "Fine. Pick Tony up and drag his ass upstairs. I'll deal with you all later."

"Yes boss."

Out of her blurred vision, she saw the outlines of the two men picking an arm each and dragging their unconscious comrade around her. She heard the fat one wheezing as he strained with the effort, followed by the sound of shoes scraping across the floor. She could feel the warm drip of blood along her temple, and saw the room around her coming in and out of focus.

Suddenly, she was flipped onto her back, and she felt the stream of blood change direction, now slowly edging towards her hairline. He was standing over her, simply watching her, studying her. She could see his chest rising and falling as she blinked back the blood from her right eye. He seemed so calm, as if this was perfectly normal.

Kneeling beside her, he began to move the hair away from her face, before caressing her cheek. His hand then moved slowly down her throat, and over her chest, fondling her breast. She pushed at his hand, and hit out at his face, before he pointed the gun at her head. It was so close, she could almost see inside the barrel. She immediately dropped her hands to her sides, her breathing quickening as he lowered it slowly until the muzzle pressed against her forehead. She closed her eyes tight, unable to stare at that gun any longer.

She again felt his hands moving over her breasts, fondling them with a gentleness not fitting the circumstances. He continued to move his hand downwards, sliding it over her stomach, then her crotch, moving between her legs. She felt like she was going to vomit, like every nerve in her body was rejecting his touch. She wanted so desperately to fight him off, to get him away from her, but she knew to do so would end in instant death. She had to hang on, she had to stay alive. Malcolm would come for her, he would be looking for her now. She just had to stay strong.

As he began to pull at her underwear, she knew he would rape her, just like he had raped Linda. She kept her eyes closed tight, trying to block out what was happening, as if to see it would make it real. She heard him undoing his belt, his zip, and the fear and grief rose in her chest. She wanted to cry out, to wail, but she wouldn't give him the satisfaction of her anguish, she refused to let him know her despair. You have to be strong.

A single tear forced its way through her tightly closed eyes and slowly made its way across her cheek, and into her hair, merging with the blood. And as she felt his weight bare down on her, she thought of Malcolm, and she prayed she would see him again.

They stayed in that office for hours, yelling, cursing, crying. It had been one of the hardest nights of Marie's life. Malcolm went over every sordid detail of his life, over and over. She insisted on knowing it all. It was like an open wound, a scab she couldn't stop picking, until it bled again. In the morning, exhausted, she'd gone to bed feeling like the wound would never close. She didn't even know what happened to the man in her kitchen. When she emerged from the office, there was no trace he'd ever existed, not so much as a single drop of blood. But every time she closed her eyes, she saw him there, begging for her help, bloodied and desperate. It made her vomit more than once that night.

She had fallen into a fitful sleep, absent of any real rest, but filled with nightmares. She dreamt of sitting at breakfast with Malcolm while he laughed and ate pancakes, except he had no skin on his face, the muscle and tendons visible, blood oozing onto his plate, and of bloodied hands reaching out to her from the shadows, dragging her away into the darkness. When she woke, her head was pounding and she felt even more tired, even more confused.

Malcolm didn't come near the room, but occasionally she would hear the creak of the floorboards outside the door, the pacing footsteps of a man contemplating a decision, before inevitably walking away again. It broke her heart. She wanted so badly to erase the night before, for him to have woken up beside her as they always had, for everything to be the way it was before. But it could never go back now.

She laid there the entire day and the next night, absorbed in her deliberations, piecing together a mass of jumbled thoughts. She hadn't called the Police, nor had she left. Both were strong indications that she wanted to stay. But could she really live that life? She had always considered herself to be a good person. Surely, turning a blind eye to something like this was tantamount to tacit approval? Surely, the blood would stain her hands as well?

But the simple fact was, she loved him. She loved him so much that even now, after all the revelations and discoveries about his true nature, after seeing just a fraction of the blood he had spilled, she still couldn't bring herself to walk away. She'd felt like half a person before Malcolm, going through the motions of life rather than enjoying it. He made her whole, and the idea of losing the other half of herself was too much to bare. She tried to picture a life without him, and it seemed to her like no life at all.

Then there was everything they'd been through together over the past few months. She had gone to the brink of death and back, and Malcolm never left her side, not once. She could never give him a child, something that meant the world to him. A world he had willingly given up for her. She knew it wasn't the same thing. After all, that had been a tragic set of circumstances beyond her control, whereas this was all done by Malcolm through his own choices, his own deliberate actions. But when she thought of the sacrifice he made for her, she wondered what she would be willing to give up for him. Her own morals perhaps? Her own beliefs? The fact was, those things paled in comparison to her life, and she knew in her heart she would willingly give hers up for him in a heartbeat if she had to, and that he would do the same for her.

She thought about the man in the chair, about the other lives taken by Malcolm over the years. Could she really live with herself if she allowed that to continue? The biggest realisation in the hours of contemplation was this: She had witnessed a man being severely beaten, and she had done absolutely nothing about it. She'd been so caught up in her own life, in the idea of losing Malcolm, of him having deceived her, of her own selfish hurt, that she had forgotten him almost the moment she entered that room. She only thought of him again the next morning when she climbed the stairs, searching for a sign of the previous night's events. She never called the Police. She never told Malcolm he had to let him go. She never bargained for his life or offered her own. He had pleaded with her to help him, he had begged her, and she had done absolutely nothing. He was most likely dead now, and she had done nothing to stop it. Perhaps, she wasn't as good a person as she thought she was. Perhaps, Malcolm and she were not so different after all.

"I'll stay."

"Oh God, baby I..."

"I never want to know anything about that part of your life. You keep it separate from me, from us, alright?"

"Of course."

"That means you can never bring it here, Malcolm. It can never enter our home again. Do I make myself clear?"

"Yes, yes...absolutely."

"And if, at some point, I change my mind. If it gets too much for me, or I can't do it anymore, you let me go. You let me walk away without a word. No trying to make me stay, or changing my mind, you simply say goodbye and that's it. Ok?"

"I... I've already taken care of that. Here." He handed her a sheet of paper, details of a bank account in Marie's name, with a one-million-pound balance.

"What is this?"

"The account is in your name, under your details. I can't access it. If you choose to leave now, or decide to down the line, I'll understand, and I won't stop you, but at least this way, I know you will be taken care of."

"Malcolm, I don't want your money, that's never been a reason for me being with you."

"I know that. I wouldn't be with you at all if that was the case. I just want you to know that I wouldn't blame you for leaving. I want to give you the means to make a fresh start, even if it is without me. And like you said, it may be that you leave now or down the line, either way this money will always be there if you need it. But if you stay Marie, if you stay, I will spend the rest of my life making you happy. I will dedicate myself to making you smile. I love you, you know that don't you?" Those three words were so powerful, they seemed to erase everything else. They seemed to justify so much.

"I know...I love you too."

He held her silently for hours, the gravity of her decision, and the reality of what it meant, weighing heavily on them both. To Marie it boiled down to one thing, and one thing only; they completed one another, and nothing on this earth could tear them apart.

Chapter Twenty Seven
- Present Day

Even though the flames had long since been extinguished, the unmistakable smell of charred flesh and acrid smoke permeated the air.

Fraser stared at the Police cordon tape blowing in the wind, dancing to the sound of sirens and raised voices. When they had traced Marie's phone, still active, to the waterside, he feared the worst. He pictured her floating on the water, her hair spread out and moving with the laps of the tide, her eyes wide and frozen with fear. He had vomited the second they arrived and found the car ablaze, barely managing to call for fire service and back up in a garbled, retching voice. He recalled reading an article on human survival instincts back at Police college. It said there were only two smells which a human could identify outside context, or without them having been previously identified and explained, and those were decomposing flesh and burning flesh. Apparently this was evolutionary, both being an indication of possible danger, or perhaps a predator nearby. The article was right. He'd been to plenty of sudden deaths and scenes, but this was the first time he had ever smelled a burning body. It was instantly recognisable and putrid to inhale, the vomit still sitting at the base of his throat, threatening to force itself free once again.

The car was still too hot to get to, and the boot was locked shut. He prayed she wasn't in there, that this ash and metal cage was not her final resting place, that the blackened flesh he smelled did not belong to her. He vomited again, just missing the feet of his Detective Inspector.

"Jesus Duncan, you'd almost think this was your first rodeo. What the hell's got into you?"

"I think I must have inhaled some of the smoke, that's all."

"Do you need to go? Tell me now before you puke all over my crime scene. I don't want to have to explain to the Chief why your DNA was found splattered all over the evidence."

Inspector Young was not what you would call a patient woman. She was twenty-two years into a thirty-year career, and in that time she'd seen and done it all. She didn't tolerate time wasters or suffer fools gladly. Fraser liked her. She looked younger than her years, her hair dyed blonde, always tied back in an elastic. She dressed plainly, like a typical detective, all dark trouser suits and beige macs. When he had moved to CID, he wondered if they'd all been provided with a clothing guide, 'How to dress like you're on a typical Police television show.'

"No, it's fine. I'm fine."

"They found the phone over there?" She pointed to a concrete bollard, thick metal chain stretching from it to the next, marking the water's edge.

"Yeah. It was sitting on top of it, still turned on."

"They obviously wanted us to find her. The husband aware we found it yet?"

Fraser thought about Malcolm, about how he would react if she was in that car, or floating nearby. He knew there would be many more bodies to come. "Not yet. I wanted to wait until we found her, until we knew for certain she was..." He trailed off, too afraid to say it out loud, just in case that would be enough to make it happen, to make it real.

The Inspector noticed, staring at him a moment, studying his face. She was not easily fooled, and was renowned for her uncanny ability to read people like a book. He heard that on one particular case, when she was still a constable, the department was dealing with the death of a ten-year-old child. Everyone liked the neighbour for it, and all the forensic evidence pointed squarely towards his guilt, but she refused to accept it, adamant it was the girl's parents who had killed her. Even after they charged the neighbour, she kept insisting they had missed something. Sure enough, a week later, they had been caught trying to burn their blood stained clothing and admitted everything in an interview. Everyone was in shock. How had she had known it was them? How, when they had been so convincing in their grief, had she seen right through them? She explained that they never used the girl's name. Even in the press appeal, and in the statements they had said their 'daughter' their 'little girl' but never Eliza. She said it was as if they were already trying to forget her, forget what they had done, that saying her name would overwhelm them with guilt. After that case, every officer in the building asked for her advice on difficult cases.

Staring him down now, it was apparent she had read him just as easily, and now realised that Marie was not just another missing person to Fraser.

"Detective Duncan..."

He almost visibly flinched when she said this. She never called him 'Detective' anything unless he was in trouble. It was like your mother using your full name.

"Inspector?"

"Is there anything I need to know about this case, about this girl, that isn't in the files or official reports?"

"No Inspector, nothing I can think of."

She continued to watch him a moment, unblinking, and for a second he thought she would call him out on the lie, expose him for his shaky alliance with Malcolm Carter, or for the deeply felt love he had for the man's wife, and sheer panic over her whereabouts now. When a slightly soot smudged uniformed Constable approached them, he was grateful for the interruption.

"Inspector, sorry to interrupt, but we managed to get the boot open. She's not inside. The teams out on the boats have finished their initial sweep and they have nothing either, so just the two male bodies so far."

Fraser felt a wave of relief, followed by the now familiar pangs of worry and fear. Relief that she was not burned up inside that car. Relief she wasn't floating in the water nearby. Fear because that meant she was still with Savage. God knows what she was going through, he dreaded to think.

"Thank you, Constable. Tell the teams everything gets rushed through the lab. Every second counts in this case. If she's still alive, we need to find her as soon as possible."

The 'if' spoken so casually in that sentence stabbed at Fraser's chest like a hot knife, but he knew better than to show his feelings this time. He turned away from them both, faking a phone call. As he walked out of ear shot, he could almost feel the Inspector's eyes burning holes in the back of his skull, but he didn't dare turn around.

He was just approaching the edge of the cordon when he heard the screeching of tyres, as a black sports car with tinted windows barely managed to stop in time, ending up just inches from the front of a marked Police car. It appeared the jungle drums had been in operation, and Malcolm had found out about the scene. Fraser braced himself for a fight.

"You can't go in there sir, it's a crime scene."

"Get me Detective Duncan, now!"

"The Detective is busy at present, but I can certainly pass on a message or..."

"Listen to me you jumped up little shit. You see that smoking wreck over there? That used to be my car. You see the bodies inside? Those were my employees, my friends. And the woman you are so incompetently searching for, well that would be my wife. So you can understand why a fucking message just isn't going to cut it. Get me Detective Duncan NOW!"

"It's ok Paul, let him though."

It had only been a couple of hours since they had forged their tenuous alliance, but Malcolm already looked like a different man. Instead of the usual polish and sheen, he looked crazed, dishevelled and sweaty. Clearly he had had as much luck with his 'enquiries' as Fraser had with his own, and he was obviously unhappy at being left out of the loop about the car.

"Mr. Carter, we can talk in here."

Fraser pointed to a mobile command centre used for large scale scenes, a large van kitted out with a few computers, main set radios and some very basic lab equipment. The two CSIs inside seemed relieved to get a break from their packaging, and with the door closed at least this afforded them a small amount of privacy. It wasn't ideal, but in a full scale Police operation, it was the best they had.

Fraser barely had time to lock the door before Malcolm had him pinned against it, both hands clutching at his shirt and jacket, his full weight pressing against him.

"I should fucking kill you." Malcolm's face was so close to his he could feel his warm, moist breath as he spat every word out.

"Let me go Malcolm. You're no good to Marie sitting inside a cell."

He could see Malcolm pondering this, the satisfaction of punching him versus the prospect of arrest. In the end, logic won out, but Fraser could see it took every ounce of strength Malcolm had not to go to town on him, then and there.

"You should have contacted me."

"And told you what? She isn't here, and we're no closer to finding her."

The words hung heavy in the air, the ramifications of what that could mean for Marie requiring no further explanation.

"I had to hear from a source, for fuck sake. She's MY wife Duncan, don't forget that."

"This is exactly why I hadn't called you yet. You're too emotional."

"And you're not?"

The truth was, he was breaking apart inside, tortured by the images of the already dead from the hundreds of Police photographs and scenes, as well as imagined images of Marie, the might be dead, the please don't be dead. He would never give Malcolm the satisfaction of knowing that.

"I'm a Police officer. I can't afford to be emotional."

Malcolm didn't seem to believe him, but he appeared too tired, too overwhelmed with worry to argue the point. "What do we know?"

"The identifications aren't formal yet, we'll need to wait for dental records to come through, but they're definitely your boys. The car was engulfed in flames before we got here, so I doubt there's any real forensic evidence inside. The only thing we found untouched by the fire was her phone. He switched it back on an hour ago, left it a few yards from the car."

"He wanted us to find it. He wants us to know he has her, and that she's next."

"Yes, that would be my guess."

Both men remained silent then, allowing themselves a moment where their worst fears and pain overwhelmed them.

"Look, we are rushing everything through, but it looks like they left nothing for us."

"Would you have expected them to?"

"No. The fact that he wanted us right here, jumping through his hoops, I doubt there's a single shred of forensic evidence to find. With Savage, there never is."

"What about searches? What about Savage's properties?"

"It wasn't easy, but based on the ongoing power struggle between you and him we managed to get warrants for the properties we know about, but so far nothing. We were expected at all of them, the smug bastard even had staff waiting for us to show up. He has so many dummy companies and friends, we are just chasing our tails. We can seek bank records, follow the money, but he knows by the time we do that she'll be..." He couldn't finish the sentence; the thought was just too painful.

Malcolm sniggered, the disturbing laugh of a man close to breaking point. "And you wonder why people don't bother coming to you anymore? This is it? The full force of Scotland Yard, the Metropolitan Police, the British justice system and you have nothing, nada, zip. It's pathetic."

Fraser could feel himself becoming defensive. "There's procedures. These things take time..."

"She doesn't have time!" Angry tears glinted in Malcolm's eyes, the sheer desperation he felt painted plainly across his face.

Fraser felt it to. In a million years he never would have believed he could have something in common with a man like Malcolm Carter, but here they both were, united in grief. United in love.

"What do you want me to do?"

"I've tried all my sources; I've hit every seedy bar or drug den Savage is associated with. I've bribed, I've blackmailed, I've spilled blood, and I have nothing. If he has her, only a very select few know where. I need to know who his top boys are. I need to know where they live, where their families live, where they buy their clothes, everything."

"What for?"

"You know damn well what for."

"You're asking me to give you, a known murderer and all round piece of shit, the entire contents of a year's investigation so I can be complicit in the assault, if not murder, of another human being? You really are something else."

"Finding them is the key to finding Marie."

"Don't you think I've thought of that already? Do you think I would leave any stone unturned for her? Detectives are already bringing them in."

Malcolm laughed again, this time loud and long. He seemed to Fraser to be somewhere between deranged and manic. He braced himself, ready for a fight.

"Bringing them in? Bringing them in? You really do have an overinflated ego, Detective. Do you really believe that your 'procedures' your 'codes' and 'policies' will save her? That you'll do such an amazing job at your paperwork that you'll save the day, swooping in at the last minute to rescue the damsel in distress and collect your commendation? WAKE UP! This is the real world. The good guys don't win. Justice? There is no justice. How many times have you poured your heart into a case for the scumbag to walk free? Or worse, to be found guilty only to walk out with a slap on the wrist? That revolving door you call a court house is meaningless to people like me. You keep ticking your boxes and fighting the good fight along that thin blue line of yours, meanwhile we fight as dirty as we like, and every time you LOSE! You lose, Detective. Except this time, if you lose, she's dead. You hear me? She's dead, and her blood is smeared all over that rule book you hold so dear."

Fraser felt the words hit him like a punch to the chest. He wanted to argue, to defend the law, to stand up for the system, but in his heart, deep down, he knew that in his own warped way, Malcolm was right. The system was failing. It was failing the Victims, it was failing the Police, it was failing Marie. He had seen it so many times over the years. How many guilty men had walked free because of a lack of prison cells, because of budgetary constraints and judges with their hands tied? How many Victims had turned to him for help, been promised every resource, everything he had, only to be let down at the last second? How many times had he choked out the words, "I'm sorry, but there's nothing we can do"? He saw the faces of so many Victims crying in the courts, of family members devastated as the sheet was pulled back to reveal the cold, blank face of their loved ones found too late, the faces of everyone who had ever put their faith in the system, their faith in him, only to be let down. They faded and reformed again behind his eyelids, mixed amongst the crime scene photos of Savage's victims, of blood and flesh and bone. And he saw Marie. Her smile, her eyes, and it broke him. What if, for once, he did play dirty? What if he broke some rules this time? Was it so wrong if it meant saving a life, if it meant saving Marie? Would he, could he do that, for her? He knew the answer before the question had even fully formed in his mind. "Ok...We'll do it your way."

When the music started, every nerve Marie felt, every doubt suddenly evaporated. This is it. "Do I look alright?"

Mickey stared at her with tears brimming, pride shining from his eyes. "I think you're the most beautiful thing I've ever seen, Miss."

She smiled, pulling him in for a hug. He had overdone it with the aftershave somewhat, and his black suit jacket strained under the width of his broad shoulders, the button almost at breaking point, his hair greased down with some kind of gel. This was Mickey in all his finest.

"Okay then, let's go."

The doors opened, revealing the inside of Capone's in all its usual splendour, the addition of hundreds of small lanterns and fairy lights giving the room a festive atmosphere. There were flowers everywhere, all white and red, and the band played 'It Had to Be You' as she walked in. This wasn't what she had originally planned; fate intervened and that wedding had to be cancelled, but as she entered the place where she first met Malcolm, as she made her way towards him, she realised this was better.

There were only a handful of guests – Linda and Richard, Mickey of course, and Sara and Charlie, who had surprised Marie the night before, making the trip over especially for the wedding. As she walked towards them, smiles lighting their faces, Sara mouthed 'I Love you' silently, blowing Marie a kiss as tears filled her eyes. She had never felt more beautiful. As she approached Malcolm however, he never turned around, and always looked front. When she finally reached him, her hand softly sliding into his, he turned to her, his face filled with pride, his eyes welling with tears, and for a moment it felt like they were the only two people in the world.

They danced, and drank champagne, Mickey cried and everyone laughed. It was the happiest day of Marie's life.

"I have a surprise for you."

He placed a blindfold over her eyes, and with a few near misses, managed to get her safely into the back of their car.

"Where are you taking me?"

"If I told you that it wouldn't be much of a surprise. I'm giving you your wedding present, so no peeking!"

She listened to the sound of traffic outside the car, of the tyres changing from a smooth surface to gravel or stones. She felt every turn, every stop, determined to savour every moment of that day, of their day.

"Malcolm?"

"No you can't take the blindfold off and no I won't tell you where we are going."

"No, I just wanted to ask you something. Wh
didn't you turn around?"

"When?"

"Today, as I was walking up the aisle. Wh
didn't you turn to look at me coming?"

"Oh I see. Honestly, I couldn't. I couldn'
because I knew the moment I did, the moment I saw
how beautiful you looked, I would lose it completely.
The truth is, I didn't want to blubber in front of
everyone." She smiled, sliding her hand across the
leather seat seeking his. He grabbed it, and squeezed
it gently, before twiddling with the wedding ring that
now sat proudly on her left hand. When they
eventually stopped, he opened the door, the chilly air
causing her bare arms to goose pimple. She felt stones
beneath her shoes.

"Where are we?"

He pulled the blindfold open and she saw
before her the most beautiful house she had ever seen.
She looked around and recognised she was in
Kensington.

"Welcome to our new home, Mrs. Carter!"

"Are you serious?"

"I'm always serious."

"Malcolm, this is too much..."

"No, this house, this day, it's a fresh start, for
both of us. The first day of our new lives together."

"I don't know what to say."

"You don't have to say anything; you already
said 'I Do', and by doing so you've made me the
happiest man in the world. I Love you Marie."

She threw her arms around his neck and kissed him passionately. Every doubt, every niggling worry about the choice she had made evaporated with each step down the aisle. She felt overwhelmed with love, with happiness, and in that moment she knew for certain that nothing would make her leave Malcolm. She would sooner die.

Chapter Twenty Nine
-Present Day

The vomit still tasted fresh in his mouth, the smell mixing with the dregs from a nearby drain. He wanted to find her just as much as Malcolm, if not more so, but this? This went against everything he stood for. What they had done to that man was so wrong, even the memory of it made him physically sick. Yet here he was, standing outside, allowing it to continue. It was his fault, all of it. He had been so desperate to save Marie, to be with her again, that he never even considered the consequences, he never even thought about where this path would lead. And then it occurred to him, maybe he had known, subconsciously? Maybe on some level, he knew and yet he still did it. For a brief moment the thought that perhaps Malcolm and him weren't so different after all flitted into his mind, and was immediately dismissed, leaving a repugnant residue lingering behind. He was different, because it made him sick, because this was a one off in extreme circumstances. This wasn't him, this wasn't who he was. For Malcolm this was his bread and butter. Inflicting pain was his pastime. They were two completely different people. He kept repeating it again and again inside his mind. I'm nothing like him.

After their discussion in the van, Fraser had made his excuses to the Inspector, the vague promise of 'following leads' and 'speaking to informants' leaving his lips a little too easily for his liking. Still, she'd looked at him the way she had on multiple occasions after he told fictitious stories of why he was 'too sick' to come to work, when in fact he was hungover, or the old 'I'm almost finished' for files that were coming worryingly close to their statute barred dates, when in fact they had simply slipped his mind. It was like she was a bloodhound whose special gift was to sniff out lies. She stared at him with that same exacting look, and for a moment he thought she had somehow read his mind, invaded his thoughts and would expose him as the traitor he was fast becoming. But after a moment, she simply said, "Okay" before hastily adding, "Don't do anything I wouldn't do." The words, said like a joke with a barb, sent a shiver down his spine. She knew something was wrong, but the saving grace was she clearly didn't know what, and that was enough to save him from accusation and exposure. Still, he would have to be very careful around her in the near future, just in case. Lies have a habit of adding up, piece by piece, until they form the whole picture, the entire jigsaw puzzle. He'd caught many men that way himself, and he would learn from their mistakes.

He travelled in his own car, with Malcolm following several car lengths behind, until they reached a building site on the edge of the city. There were no CCTV cameras or prying eyes through twitching curtains here.

"There's a lad who does a lot of running around for Savage, almost like a personal assistant to a psychopath. He picks up the rope, the tape, the hack saws. We have receipts and CCTV of him buying the goodies for his boss, but nothing more concrete than that. We have a few photos of him with Savage, some phone records of calls, but nothing is ever said that would help us. We had him in earlier, he gave us nothing as usual. Just a load of shit about being a painter/decorator for Savage. I reckon if anyone knows where she is, it's him."

"Name?"

The tone was demanding. It got Fraser's back up almost immediately. "Listen Carter, you aren't in charge here. If you want my help, you follow my rules, got it?"

Malcolm smiled that sinister smile, the same one he made when he spotted the Police photographers following him. "Whatever you say, Detective."

He emphasised the word detective, almost inferring he was a fraud or a fake, but Fraser didn't have time to argue right now. "His name is Neil Blair. Savage and his men call him Neily. He lives on the same estate Savage grew up on."

"We had looked at Blair as a possible source, but he seemed small fish."

"He is, that's the point. He's thick as pig shit, but he's also a childhood friend, so Savage keeps him around out of some sense of loyalty. He does nothing but grunt work, lifting and laying, nothing more but he works under the illusion that he's one of the big boys, and they're happy to let him think it as long as he does his bit."

"Ok, so you think he may have done some grunt work for this particular job, for Marie?"

The sound of her name uttered from such unworthy lips made Fraser tense up. He hated that she was bound to this man, that she had been taken in by his charm and lies. He wanted nothing more than to hit him, hard, but this wasn't the time. He couldn't help rescue Marie from Malcolm until he saved her from Savage, and as distasteful as it was, for that to happen he would have to make a deal with the devil.

"Exactly. Savage must have been watching Marie for a while, working out her movements, the routes your boys took. They knew exactly where she would be and when."

"You mean, when she was meeting you?"

He found his body tensing again, his teeth gritted and grinding together. Malcolm clearly couldn't help himself. Fraser pictured going to town on his face, knocking his teeth out. He had done a bit of amateur boxing back in the day, and given half a chance, he would turn Malcolm's pretty face into mush. He had to keep telling himself this wasn't the time. 'Later, later' was his internal monologue. "My point is, he has been preparing for this for a while. He would have had a location to take her, and items he needed. He favours gaffer tape and the plastic sheeting painters use to protect floors, something you two have in common I think?"

He couldn't help giving a dig back. The hate felt between them was almost visible now, a thick, rancid fog permeating around each man. Fraser realised how precarious the alliance was. One insult too many, one push too far, and one of the men was bound to snap. He was suddenly very aware of the fact that he was alone, without back up or anyone knowing where he was, with Malcolm and two of his goons, in a very remote part of town. He felt adrenaline beginning to surge through his veins.

But Malcolm just smiled that same wry smile that drove Fraser mad. "Indeed...I think it's about time we paid Mr. Blair a visit, don't you?"

It hadn't been difficult to find him. Fraser accessed Savage on the database and searched for his associates and the locations they frequented. Within one hour, they found Neil Blair at his sister's address, forcing him into the car boot before driving to an old auto repair shop belonging to Malcolm.

The shutters on the front had graffiti, the tags of a dozen or so kids, marking the territory of an area no one wanted, a shop long forgotten. Inside, the air was stale and it smelled of engine oil. In the centre of the room stood the body of an old Ford, its engine parts removed, like the carcass of a once great beast long since picked apart by vultures. Fraser wasn't sure what irritated him more; the fact that Malcolm had been the one to grab and detain Neily, or that Fraser, despite all of his investigations and enquiries into every detail of Malcolm's life, had no idea that he owned this building. A small, and slightly narcissistic part of him, believed Malcolm brought them here, to this hidden spot, just to taunt him.

There were multiple chains hanging from the ceiling, once used as a pulley system for heavy car parts, now forgotten and covered in black grease and dust. Neily was placed with his hands above his head, hanging from the chain most central in the room. It instantly reminded Fraser of the paintings he'd seen depicting the Spanish inquisition.

Neily was a tall, lanky man, with sharp features and greasy black hair. In fact, all of him was greasy, his face constantly reflecting the light. He smelled strongly of overpriced aftershave, and body odour, and his grey tracksuit showed two large sweat patches under his arms, creeping slowly across his chest, as if they were trying to meet in the middle. His eyes were wide with fear, darting about the room at all of those inside, going from face to face, asking for help and receiving none. Fraser stayed out of the way where he wouldn't be seen. After this was over, he never wanted to be associated with what happened here. He never wanted this to come back on him, a thought which was indicative of how wrong it all was.

"You know who I am, don't you Mr. Blair?"

He nodded wildly, almost desperately, as if the right answer may act as some kind of password to freedom.

"Then you know what I am capable of? What I am more than willing, no, more than happy to do to you in order to get the answers I want?"

He nodded again, this time more slowly, cautiously.

"Well then, I'll make it very simple. Tell me where my wife is and I will let you live."

Neily stared at him, his eyes welling up, seeking an answer he was afraid to give. Suddenly, Malcolm made a quick movement towards him, punching him hard across his right cheek, sending blood and saliva through the air. Neily cried out in pain. Fraser flinched, a reflexive move, every part of his training, of his conscience telling him to stop it before it went too far. But it was momentary. He knew this was inevitable, and so he remained out of sight, grateful it wasn't him who had to do the dirty work.

"Please don't make me ask again, Mr. Blair."

"Please, please...I can't! He'll kill me!"

"Well then it appears you have a problem, Mr. Blair. If you tell me, he will kill you, and if you don't, I will. And trust me, it will not be quick."

Again, Fraser flinched at the word 'kill'. He had expected violence, and torture, but murder? That wasn't what they agreed on. But a sudden realisation fell over him like a shadow; there were no terms and conditions to this gentleman's agreement of theirs. There was only two desperate men trapped in a desperate coalition. He couldn't let that happen. He wouldn't. But then, how could he stop it?

"Please, I'm begging you..."

Another blow, again across his face, spraying more blood and sending Neily's head bouncing like a rag dolls. Fraser began to feel the bile rising in his throat. He had watched boxing matches, he had pulled apart a hundred drunken fights outside pubs on a Saturday night, but this violence was so different. It was more brutal, more cruel. He shifted his focus from the victim to the perpetrator, and was amazed at just how calm he seemed. He was literally torturing another human being who hung from the ceiling like the remains of a cow in a butcher's freezer, yet he looked as if he could be doing his taxes, only the faint sheen of perspiration revealing the physical exertion of the activity. Only his eyes revealed his despair, his anguish, at the thought of losing her.

"I'm beginning to lose patience, Mr. Blair. Where is she?"

"P-P-Please..."

Malcolm removed a flick knife from his pocket, its silver blade glinting even in this dull light as he released it from the tortoise shell handle. He placed it against Neily's ear, his hand steady despite the implication of what was happening. Neily began to struggle, pulling his head frantically away from the blade, flailing wildly against the chains which bound him. Without a word, the two men who had accompanied Malcolm walked over, one grabbing Neily's legs and the other his upper body, holding him steady. Malcolm too grabbed hold of him, except he went for the head, clutching Neily's greasy hair between his fingers, holding his head in place as he sliced into his ear, hacking and sawing until it was detached from his face. Blood streamed down the side of his face, and he cried out, a deep, tortuous howl.

It took a second for Fraser to register what was happening, but when it did, the bile began to rise ever closer to the surface, threatening to burst through at any moment. He watched Malcolm discard the ear like a sweet wrapper, tossing it to the side. It left a small red stain where it sat, and Neily stared at it as he cried to himself the way a child would when they are injured.

"Every time you don't answer me, I will slice a bit of you off. Do you understand? Where is she?"

Neily just continued to cry, failing to make any attempt to answer the question. Perhaps the fear, the shock, had rendered him mute, or perhaps he could no longer hear well having lost three quarters of his right ear, but either way the lack of response did nothing to placate Malcolm. He lunged toward Neily, this time the knife aimed at the tip of his nose. Fraser couldn't stand it anymore, and he managed to grab Malcolm's arm just as he had begun to draw blood.

"I won't let you kill him!"

They just stayed there a moment, all four of them around the weeping, bloody boy, puppeteers in a grotesque marionette show. Malcolm looked angry at first, the men, releasing their grips from their victim, all of them staring at Fraser with intense, dark eyes. For a moment, he thought his colleagues would be pulling him out of the river next. But Malcolm laughed instead. It was a natural laugh, almost too casual for the situation they found themselves in. A man at a play, laughing at a tragedy. It took them all by surprise, even his goons. He freed his arm from Fraser's grip, but kept the knife visible, and in his hand, a clear indication of what he could do if he so chose. Fraser kept eye contact with Malcolm, the knife sitting on the edge of his peripheral vision; a silent and ever present threat.

"Don't worry, Detective. I won't kill him. Despite what you might think of me, what your psychological profilers have written in their reports, I am not a psychopath. I don't take a man's life unless it is absolutely necessary, and it won't be in this case, I can assure you. Mr. Blair will come to his senses. It might take a pound of his flesh, but he'll tell me exactly what I need to know, and then he will stumble out of London forever. Because he knows if he stays, whether it's by my hand or Savage's, he'll lose more than his ear. Isn't that right, Mr. Blair?"

Neily just continued to cry quietly, a wounded animal, cornered and outnumbered by predators.

Fraser stayed where he was, unsure how to react. "Do you want to find her or not?" Fraser stepped backwards, moving slowly away from the man he had just tried to save, and the man who could kill him.

Malcolm smiled. "That's what I thought." And with that he reached up and began to saw at one of Neily's fingers, blood surging from the wound, the sound of flesh giving way to steel. The men resumed their positions and Neily continued his gurgled, frantic cries.

It was all too much for Fraser. He stumbled out of the building, slamming into the shutters as he went, the sound of metal unable to drown out the yells. He barely got outside before he emptied the contents of his stomach, the acidic bile stinging his nostrils. He sank against the shutters, feeling them buckle slightly under his weight as he slid down onto the dirty ground, inches from his own vomit. There were no sounds out here, but he could still hear the cries, the pleas, inside his head. They echoed and bounced around, giving him a headache worse than any he had ever felt before. He could feel the pulse in his neck, the artery pumping as hard as it could. He felt as if it would burst at any moment, that his blood would be spilled too. Karma for the blood being spilled inside.

He closed his eyes and thought of Marie, of finding her alive, but the image of Neily, of a piece of flesh which used to be an ear in a small bloody puddle, kept popping into his mind. He swallowed hard, trying to prevent a second bout of sickness. I am nothing like him.

After what seemed like an eternity, Malcolm emerged wiping his hands with an old oil stained rag, the red refusing to mix with the ancient black stains. He looked at Fraser, clammy and nauseous on the pavement, and then the pile of partially digested food and bile nearby. For a moment he said nothing, and just continued to rub his fingers, cleaning spots of blood that no longer stained his hands. When he spoke, it was calm and controlled, as if a great weight had been lifted, as if everything that just occurred had never happened, and this was just a casual conversation between strangers.

"She's at an old disused pub building on the outskirts of the city. I have the address, and I've wired off my guys. Neily says there are about half a dozen of Savage's boys there, armed to the teeth, so we'll need back up and weapons. And Fraser..." he looked up at Malcolm, their eyes fixed on each other. "...She's alive." A huge wave of relief poured over Fraser. She was alive. Marie was alive, and soon they would save her, soon he would be with her again. A niggling thought edged into his mind. "What about Neily?"

Malcolm smirked, looking down at his hands as he continued to wipe them with the cloth. "He's alive, too. A little worse for wear, and missing a few pieces, but he'll live."

As Malcolm stepped back into the shadows of the partially shuttered doorway, Fraser felt his heart pounding in his chest. She was alive, so surely everything had been worth it? I am nothing like him. I am nothing like him.

Chapter Thirty
-One Year Ago

"Detective Duncan, I presume?"

Fraser started at the mention of his name. He'd had a long night unpacking and with only a few hours' sleep, and nearly a fifty minute wait for the early senior management meeting to end, he had just dosed off in the orange plastic chair which, along with its blue companion, created a make shift waiting area in the corridor outside the Inspector's office.

He shot out of the chair, straightening his tie as he did so in some feeble attempt to look more alert. She smiled at him, clearly amused at having disturbed his dosing.

"Apologies for the delay. We had two homicides last night, both gang related. Senior management are shitting their pants as usual."

He couldn't hide his surprise at her blunt phrasing, her brutal honesty. It was something he wasn't used to in a boss. She smiled that same amused smile again. Nothing gets past you does it? She motioned towards the door beside them, a black plastic sign declaring this to be the office of 'Inspector Young, Organised Crime.' He stepped inside what was a surprisingly chaotic office. There were dozens of files and boxes, stacked here and there, with only a small area left free on the desk for the computer keyboard.

"Don't worry, it may look like a bomb went off in here, but I know where everything is. It's a filing system I devised years ago." She chuckled to herself more than to him. Before he could say anything, the phone on her desk rang. She gestured to apologise and let him know she would only be a moment. He nodded in response.

"Inspector Young..."

He took the opportunity to look at her more closely. She was older than he was, with blonde hair tied neatly back in a ponytail, and bright, alert eyes. She wore only a minimal amount of makeup, and truthfully she did not need any more. She appeared younger than he knew her to be, having googled her prior to today's meeting, and only a few small lines around her eyes seemed to betray her. She was warm and welcoming, but her quick intellect and impressive perceptive skills was apparent almost immediately, which led to Fraser feeling a little on guard, especially after the first impression he had just managed to give her.

She was wearing a plain black polar neck jumper, with simple grey suit trousers and practical black flat shoes. The only jewellery she wore was a gold band on her wedding finger and a black leather strapped watch. She gave the impression of a woman with intent, a woman to be taken very seriously.

Her office however, was not as minimalist as her clothing. The wall behind her was covered in framed photographs and certificates. He could see a degree in Criminology from the University of London, four commendations, and a photograph of her shaking hands and accepting an award from the Chief Constable himself, both grinning eagerly at the camera. There was a dubious fern in one corner, which looked like it was mere moments away from being the next death discussed at the morning meetings. Amongst the files and papers, he could see one solitary personal item, a picture of the Inspector with a grey haired man, both kneeling beside a large golden retriever.

"I expect that to be on my desk by the end of day, okay? Okay." She promptly hung up the phone with no attempt at pleasantries and refocused her attention on him. Fraser suddenly felt like he was in a job interview, despite his application having been successful and his transfer confirmed. He could feel his mouth drying up and was suddenly painfully aware of his five o'clock shadow.

"Well, Detective Duncan, how are you finding London so far?"

"Fine. Good."

"Ha, it's overpopulated and we are under-resourced. We are fighting up hill, detective."
He was reminded of a very upright General in some old black and white war movie, discussing the situation with his troops. She seemed to expect a reply, but he hadn't heard a question. "Yes, well all the emergency services are suffering with these cuts." Pathetic.

She smiled again, and although clearly not impressed by his response, she continued. "We have roughly one hundred murders a year in this city,

Detective, and smaller and smaller numbers of Officers to deal with them. These budget cuts have hit the force hard, and if it wasn't for the separate budget for gang related violence, there would be a hell of a lot more. This unit is my baby, Detective. I set her up ten years ago and I have watched her workload increase year in and year out. I need officers who can deal with the cause, not just the clean-up. Do you follow me?"

"Well, yes, of course. I have been involved in education-based programmes at my old force, in schools and..."

"What are you talking about? Education based? That's for the community officers and the plastic peelers. I'm talking about hitting these gangs at their heart, their income. I want as many of them in jail at once as possible, and not just the low lives and grunt men, I want the leaders, the bosses. I want every piece of finance poured over and every laundered pound accounted for. I want their assets seized and any illegal businesses like the drugs, the girls, shut down. I want you to make their lives as miserable as possible. Do you understand?"

"Yes Ma'am."

"Good. Head upstairs then and get started. Edwards will show you the ropes."

He paused, expecting something further, but when it became clear that his 'pep talk' was complete, he lifted himself from his chair and made his way out of the office.

"Just one more thing, Detective."

He turned in the doorway, still dazed from everything she'd already said, and having no idea what to expect next. "I've put you on the Carter case.

He's the big fish right now, and I want him out of my pond."

"Yes ma'am."

"Good stuff. Off you pop."

As he made his way toward the stairs, he thought about their conversation. He'd met plenty of Senior officers in his time, but none quite so blunt. It wasn't quite the welcome speech he had expected. He read up on the unit prior to application of course. According to the Met's website, it was an 'Elite team of specially trained officers dedicated to the investigation and reduction of gang related violence within the London Metropolitan area.' They had some successes, with many high profile murder investigations solved, and thanks to partnerships with the drugs unit, dozens of drug factories and Cannabis farms had been located and shut down, but the truth was they had barely made a dent. As the Police got better, the gangs got smarter, and with new groups springing up every day, and the Police budgets getting smaller and smaller, the tides had turned in favour of the criminals.

Carter. Malcolm Carter. He had read about him in the news a few times, a footnote in several articles, someone 'helping Police with their enquiries.' He had never been charged with anything of course, in fact Fraser didn't think he had even been arrested before. He asked a few friends in the Met who the major players were, and all of them named Carter. According to them, the few times the Police had actually managed to turn one of his men grass, whether it was through bribery, blackmail, or the promise of protection, they disappeared almost immediately only to be found a few days later in more pieces than your average jigsaw puzzle. As a result, his crew was locked up tight and leads were becoming few and far between.

After a wrong turn leading to the rec room and what appeared to be a domestic between a plain clothes officer and a uniform, he found the Organised Crime office. The door was wedged open with a fire extinguisher, hence why he had walked right past it. When he entered the room, there were people rushing back and forth amongst mountains of boxes and papers. He wondered if they learned their filing system from the Inspector. He could hear the familiar beep of the radio transmission in between garbled words, as well as an ancient radio in one corner playing what sounded like Radio two.

He thought he would take the place in a bit before finding Edwards. There were two large whiteboards on wheels, one on either side of the room. Both displayed dozens of pictures, mug shots as well as covertly captured photos, with lines spiderwebbing from each face to the next, a giant connect the dots describing a criminal organisation. One had Carter at the top, a covert picture of him in a sharp black suit and reflective sunglasses. He stared at the board trying to make sense of the pattern, the hierarchy, and familiarise himself with his new customers. Some were faces he had seen before, or names he had heard of, but most were completely unknown. The sudden realisation of starting something from nothing hit him hard, and he longed for his old desk and the familiar faces he arrested and questioned day in and day out. You wanted this. You worked for this.

He moved across to the other board. The face at the top of this web couldn't have been farther from Carter. He was much younger. Instead of a designer suit, this lad wore a navy Adidas tracksuit and matching cap. He looked like your typical scumbag, the type of kid he'd seen in the cell dozens of times, but something about him was very different. His eyes. They were cold, dead. They were the eyes of someone much older than this kid's years. The name scrawled beside the mug shot read 'Jonathan Savage.' Fraser had never heard of him, but one thing was clear, he had no difficulty recruiting. His web was much larger than Carters, with more faces staring out from the board. None of them looked over thirty and almost all of them had some ridiculous nickname, like 'Tubz' and 'DeeDee'. Fraser wondered when it became obligatory for every criminal to have a pseudonym.

"Can I help you?"

He turned to face an overweight, balding man with one of the worst comb overs he had ever seen and what appeared to be gravy on his garish baby pink tie.

"Yes, I was looking for Edwards. My name's Fraser, I'm starting with the unit today."

"Ah the transferee, Scotland right?"

Fraser thought his accent made that abundantly clear, but he just nodded politely.

"I'm Mark, Mark Haywood. I work the Savage gang." He moved his Sports Direct coffee cup to his other hand, and worryingly wiped his hand on his sweaty shirt before reaching towards Fraser.

Part of him wondered what exactly he was cleaning off, but he didn't want to be rude, so he accepted the damp hand and shook it. "Fraser Duncan, eh, from Scotland. I was told to speak to Edwards?"

"Oh yeah, he's in the corner there." He pointed his fat finger towards the desk in the furthest corner of the office before shuffling towards the coffee area near the door. Fraser just had enough time to watch him wipe his hand on his shirt again before he began fingering the box of cream buns in front of the filter. He appeared to settle on the fourth bun he poked before shoving half of it inside his mouth, and a not insignificant amount down his front. Remind me not to eat any of those.

The man at the desk had his head down, so Fraser could just see the top of his head covered in thick black hair, and his brown-skinned hand frantically scribbling across a page in front of him. He was wearing a blue striped shirt with a sky blue silk tie, and he could just make out the edge of thick rimmed, black frame glasses. Whatever he was working on, it was clearly important, as he hadn't even noticed Fraser approaching.

His desk was neater than the rest, with files stacked in colour-coordinated piles, a pea green pile to his left and a blue pile to his right. The keyboard had been shoved on top of one of the piles to allow him space to write, and apart from a plastic desk organiser containing several pens, highlighters and pencils, the only other items on his desk were a coffee stained mug reading 'World's Best Dad' and a small picture frame, the contents of which Fraser could not make out from this angle.

He stood a moment half expecting Edwards to sense his presence or notice the large shadow now cast across his desk, but after what felt like a much longer space of time than had actually passed, Fraser coughed. When that didn't work, he decided the direct approach would be best.

"Edwards? Excuse me, Edwards?"

He looked up suddenly, his large hazel eyes peering above his thick rimmed glasses. He didn't speak, appearing to expect Fraser to continue.

"Um, I'm Fraser Duncan. The Inspector told me to speak to you?"

"Oh Duncan, yes. Sorry, yes. I'm Vihaan." He stood and offered Fraser his hand, which he gratefully shook. "You're the new guy."

"Yes, I started this morning. I've been allocated the Carter case."

"Hah! If you can call it a case. Guy's Teflon. You'll be on a team with me, Clare and Tom, they're in interview at the moment. Mark over there works the Savage case." He tilted his head toward Haywood, who didn't seem to hear the mention of his name as he licked whipped cream off his tie.

"Right, we met."

"There's another three working on the Savage case with Mark, they're running a surveillance op at the moment. Him and Carter are the top dogs right now, then there's another three working on the remaining smaller gangs. Nowhere near enough to be honest, we can be stretched pretty thin, so we all chip in with each other's stuff when we can. Let me introduce you."

He led Fraser over to the board he'd been

examining and proceeded to introduce each photo with a bio of their previous convictions and role within the Carter organisation. "This is Michael Finlay, known by Mickey to his boss and colleagues. He's low level, acts mostly as a driver and body guard. He has several previous for assaults and petty crimes. He isn't the brightest, but man is he loyal. He's already done a few years for GBH on a drug dealer who tried to move into Carter's patch. He was offered complete immunity in the case if he told us Carter had ordered the beating, or hell, if he just rolled on Carter for anything, but nope. Kept his mouth shut. This boy is Richard Wallace, Carter's right hand man. He has previous for serious assaults, couple of B and E's and robbery, and some weapons charges, but most stuff bounced off him as easy as it did Carter. He's suspected in three murders, and that's just the ones we know about. Could never prove any of it, of course. He likes to use his hands, basically beats them to death. Lastly, and right at the top, we have Malcom John Carter. This boy is old school, runs his patch of London like the Mob ran America back in the day. He has his hand in everything, weapons, girls, stolen goods, some drugs, usually the lighter stuff, forgery, money laundering, fraud, blackmail, you name it, he does it. He has a number of legitimate businesses, several properties, an antiques dealership, a bar. We suspect these are used to launder the money, but haven't been able to prove a thing. Our forensic accountant poured over his books and never found a penny out of place. I honestly don't know how he does it. Then there's the violence. He is suspected of having ordered at least half a dozen murders, and believed to have personally carried out at least two."

Fraser raised his eyebrows at this, surprised a major player like Carter would get his hands dirty.

Edwards spotted it straight away. "I know what you're thinking, but he hates snitches. Rumour has it, he deals with rats personally. Once you see the case file photos, you'll understand why no one grasses on him."

He seemed to see this as a natural pause in his story, and led Fraser over to at least twenty grey filing cabinets lining the side of the room. Fraser noticed a few cut out newspaper articles taped to some of the cabinets, detailing several high profile arrests and successful convictions. One of the cabinet drawers had a full A4 sheet taped to it, with the words 'If I died and went straight to Hell, it would take me a week to realise I wasn't in work anymore', accompanied by a cartoon picture of a man weeping at his desk.

"These are the most recent investigations into Carter's crew, the older stuff is in a storage room down the hall." Fraser wondered how many filing cabinets had been filled, and how many forests lost to Carter and his boys. Edwards smiled. "Don't worry, no one expects you to read them all. I've prepared a Cliffs Notes version for your convenience."

He handed Fraser a stuffed blue folder, with a large elastic band straining to contain the papers within. "Read through that, learn the faces and names, and you'll be good to go."

Fraser removed the band and flicked to a random point in the file. He read through two pages of detailed case notes before stopping at a photograph. The subject was a young woman. He was surprised to find any women inside the folder, especially such a petite, well-groomed one. Certainly, there had been none on the board. But more than that, there was something about her that stuck with Fraser almost immediately. She had porcelain skin, jet black hair, and sad eyes. She was beautiful.

"Who's the girl?"

"Ah, that's Mrs. Carter herself, Malcolm's wife. Northern Irish, a couple of minors from when she was a juvie but nothing more. From what we can tell, she's your normal, law abiding citizen with zero involvement in the criminal activity. Hell, we've had her in a few times, tried to turn her grass, but she's loyal. I don't think she even knows what her husband does to be honest. Shame really, a nice, pretty girl like that falling prey to an animal like Malcolm Carter."

Fraser stared at the girl in the photograph. It appeared to have been taken covertly, a long angled lens through a car window. Fraser had always preferred photos taken without the knowledge of the subject. They showed the person when they weren't acting happy or faking a smile. They were honest. What he saw in Marie was a frightened young woman, another victim in a long line of victims, falling prey to monsters like Carter.

"Yes...a shame."

Chapter Thirty One
-Present Day

Marie lay on the cold hard floor and stared at the particles of dust dancing through the murky green light of the fire escape sign above her. Occasionally it would flicker, and for a moment the dust would be lost, before returning again to continue their ballet. She could hear it hum in the silence and it brought the smallest of comforts to her; it proved she was still alive.

She put her hand to her face and neck. Both felt swollen and tender, and she could feel contours created by dried blood. The beating hadn't been the worst part for her, if anything the physical violence had been a welcome break from the sexual. The thought of it made her retch, the taste of stale vomit still present in her mouth. She wasn't sure if it had been the blows to her stomach or her disgust at the things he'd done to her which made her violently ill, but either way it had been many hours since her last drink, and regurgitation only left her all the more dehydrated. She felt weaker than ever, fading in and out of consciousness, unsure upon waking if she was in a dream or the real world. The hum of that sign was what reminded her where she was.

At one point, as she walked the cusp of unconsciousness, she thought she had seen her Grandmother smiling at her. It was so vivid, she even smelled her rose water perfume and soapy shampoo. That was when she thought she must be dead, or at least dying, as if her Grandmother was an escort sent to take her from this awful nightmare to the other side. Instead, she just stood there, watching over her for a moment, before vanishing again into the concrete wall behind her. A small part wished she was dead, wished that this was over and she could feel peace again. But she was a fighter, always had been, and the truth was she was too stubborn, too strong willed, to give up.

She hadn't given him the satisfaction of her tears, or pleas, not even once. At points, when he was hitting her, he had told her to beg, but she had remained silent, answering his order with a glob of bloody spit, which hit him square in the eye before slowly edging its way down the side of his face. He stood a moment, fists clenched, teeth gritted, and she braced herself, waiting for the final blow to come. But instead, he knelt down and gripped her swollen, battered face, raising her ear towards his mouth. "I know what you're trying to do. You're trying to provoke me, trying to make me put you out of your misery. Well that won't happen, not until I've had my fun. I'm gonna make you feel so much more pain before I finally get bored of it and kill you." The words had been spat into her ear, spraying the side of her face with warm spittle and whiskey breathe. Despite her will, it was getting harder and harder to harbour hope, and slowly it faded piece by piece.

Occasionally, she would hear the creaking footsteps of heavy set men outside the door, and she would feel her body tensing, preparing itself for another round. But no one had come for a good while now. Perhaps he had had his fun? Perhaps he was making preparations to dispatch her. A memory suddenly flashed into her mind of a floor covered with plastic sheeting and a man bloodied and terrified, bound to a chair. She wanted to weep, but whether it was through dehydration or exhaustion, she didn't seem to have any tears left to shed. Maybe this is my punishment.

Malcolm was true to his word. Neily had been unceremoniously dumped at the car park of the nearest hospital, and after treatment would inevitably skip town.

They were on their way to a derelict pub in the estate where Savage grew up, which had long since closed. The outside was now covered in weathered boarding and a decade's worth of bills and posters in varying states of repair, a timeline of events in the area. At one point, it had been called 'The Deer's Head' but now through the British weather and attacks from local vandals, most of the letters of the sign had fallen or broken apart, leaving only the word 'Dead' above the door. Fraser prayed it wasn't some kind of an omen.

He thought about contacting his Inspector, of doing this legitimately and legally. But it would have raised too many questions about where he got the information and how it could be assessed to be reliable. With Neily nursing a three fingered hand and a bag of ice containing an ear, it was just too big a risk. Especially with his Inspector being a human lie detector. He would lose his job, his home, everything. Then there was the time issue. By the time they rallied together a firearms support unit and all the other back up required, planned and briefed them on the raid, and made their way to the building, Marie would probably be long since dead. No, he couldn't risk losing her. Then there was Malcolm. While he had been scrambling with call signs and superior officers, he would have carried on regardless. This was the only way he could ensure that Malcolm didn't slaughter everyone. As well as these things, a small part of him hated the idea of Malcolm rescuing her. It should be him. He would never admit it to himself, but this urge to be her hero was as big an influence on his decision as any of the other factors.

Malcolm had tried to leave without him, but Fraser insisted on being present. In other circumstances, he imagined Malcolm would have put up more of a fight, but he just sighed heavily and nodded. Both knew they were too stubborn to ever let the other 'handle it', that wasn't how either man worked, and there just wasn't any time to argue.

They pulled up around the corner, and sat a few minutes waiting on Malcolm's back up to arrive. The only sound was the clicks of the engine cooling down and Fraser's own jagged breath. He wondered if it sounded as loud to the others in the car as it did inside his own head. As they watched, a heavy set man in a burgundy tracksuit with a swollen nose and black eye had shuffled his way out of the alleyway behind the bar, before returning a short while later with two large bags from the local hardware store. Fraser tried to guess what was inside, bleach perhaps, plastic sheeting, some tools? The thought made him feel sick and he began picturing every vile situation imaginable. Perhaps she was already dead? Perhaps they were too late? No, he refused to give up on her, not until he knew for sure, not until he'd tried everything. Malcolm and Fraser looked at each other as the fat man whistled his way down the street and inside the building, the bags straining under the weight of the items inside. They knew that whatever they were going to do, it needed to happen soon.

When Marie heard the bolt shifting on the door, she flinched. He had been up and down so many times she now knew his heavy footsteps from the others, and the nausea and dread increased with every step he took towards her.

She was curled up in the darkest corner of the room, hiding behind the empty crates. She knew there was no point in hiding, not really, but the instinct to survive is so engrained in all of us, it forces us to keep going, even when it's hopeless.

"Where is my girl, hmmm?" She hated that he called her that, it literally made her skin crawl. "Are you hiding from me? Are we playing a game? I like games, it makes the prize all the sweeter when I win. We could play hide and seek? No, let's play hot and cold." She could hear the scraping of heavy items being moved, of pipes clunking together and some falling to the ground, as he made his way around the room.

"Cold...cold...am I warm yet baby?" His voice

sounded so jovial as he spoke, as if they were two friends genuinely engaged in some fun activity. Malcolm calls me baby. She felt a flood of emotion as he used the nickname that once meant so much joy to her; disgust and anger at his use of it, and sorrow over the fact that she would never again hear Malcolm call her that. She felt her skin go warm and throat swell, she wanted to cry, but instead she held her breathe, she held it in, desperate not to make the slightest sound. Anything to delay the pain. "Cold...Colder...not many places left now." She could hear him coming closer, she could almost feel him on top of her again, the weight of him suffocating her. "Cold...I have a feeling I know where you are." He would be on her any second, she only had a moment left, perhaps her last moment ever, and so she closed her eyes and pictured Malcolm. She pictured his smile, his eyes. She remembered the way his home-cooked pancakes tasted, the smell of his aftershave, the sound of him breathing as he slept beside her. "Warm....warmer..." She thought about the first time they met, the first time they kissed, the way his lips tasted. "Warmer..." She thought about their life together, of how happy they had been, and the tears started to fall. She wanted to find peace in the memories, to feel appreciation for the life she'd lead, the happy moments she had enjoyed, rather than the ones she would lose out on, but she wanted so desperately to be with him again, to make more memories with him, to see him grow old. But he found her. He had won the game, and she had no time left to regret. "Hot...Found you! Oh don't cry baby. It's almost over now. It's almost over."

Everything had been in slow motion. Fraser had run drills and exercises of emergency hostage situations, of hitting a building, but he'd never actually done it for real. Adrenaline surged through his body as he entered the building, and every inch of him felt tense and ready for a fight. But the second they stepped inside, he felt grossly underprepared. Only his love for Marie spurring him on.

One of Malcom's men had knocked on the door, and as he heard footsteps reaching it, and locks being moved, he put his full weight against the door, sending it and the man behind it flying backwards with a bang. They immediately entered what looked like a storage room, crates and boxes were stacked against the walls and the rest of the room was filled with shelves, dust covering where bottles and cans were once stored. There had only been two men inside this first room; the fat one in the burgundy tracksuit who now lay crumpled behind the door, and a tall, greasy one who stood stunned as they entered, unable to react fast enough when one of Malcolm's men hit him with a baseball bat, sending a tooth and blood flying and his body folding to the floor like a puppet whose strings had been suddenly cut.

They didn't stop, charging out to the main bar, some of Malcolm's other boys remaining behind to guard the rear door and the two unconscious males. Fraser charged through, running just behind Malcolm and the heavyset male who had ensured their entry. The door ahead led behind the bar's counter which had once been a dark polished wood, but now it was covered in graffiti, cigarette burns and dust. What at one time had been old fashioned, red damask wallpaper, was now faded a washed out orange, and it peeled away in large curls all along the walls giving the building the impression of being diseased. The red carpet had been torn up to reveal rotting floorboards, and bare wiring hung down from the ceilings at various intervals, like hands reaching through the murky light.

There were six males in here, that he could see immediately, and all of them were already running for cover when they got inside, the noise of their entrance having provided a short warning. When the first shot was fired, it narrowly missed Fraser's head, landing on the wall behind him sending plaster and dust out in swirls. Instinctively, he dived down beneath the bar. He held the crowbar tightly, twisting it in his hands. As shots continued to be fired, several of which hit the wall above him, he felt extremely vulnerable.

He could hear various thuds and wails as fights continued beyond his shelter out of his line of sight. He crawled along the ground and peered from the other side of the bar. Before he got a chance to take in what was happening, someone kicked him hard in the face. He felt pain shoot through his jaw and heard the crunch of teeth against teeth. Before his attacker had the chance to inflict a second blow, he grabbed his feet, clutching them towards his chest in a tight bear hug, before rolling onto them, forcing the male's legs to buckle under his weight and for him to fall backwards with a thud. He didn't have time to worry about the various other threats in the room, throwing his full weight onto the male. They punched each other hard, both making contact with the other, both inflicting pain, but Fraser was stronger. He punched him hard in the face, over and over, as he felt his knuckles get wet and the body beneath him go limp. He was breathing heavily, and could feel the pain in his jaw spreading around his body, the taste of copper now filling his mouth, his heartbeat audible inside his head.

He pushed himself up and heard a shot just behind him. He froze, as if for a moment he wasn't sure if he himself was hit, before a body fell to the floor to his right, a bloody hole spreading over the white baseball cap. He turned, crow bar in hand ready for a fight, when he saw Malcolm, gun still raised. It took him a moment to understand what just happened. He thought for an instant that Malcolm was betraying him, that he was getting rid of him now he had served his purpose, but he simply lowered the gun. He looked at the man beside him and saw he had a gun in his hand, and he suddenly knew Malcolm had just saved his life.

He was on top of her when the bang of a door being demolished echoed around the basement walls, and heavy footsteps and yelling spread like fire throughout the building above them. When the first shot sounded, he was already frantically doing up his belt as he ran up the steps towards the commotion. It took her a few seconds to understand what was happening, the recent punches having left her dazed, the ringing in her left ear and general drowsiness giving her the feeling of being under water. A gun shot brought her back to the now. Malcolm, he's come for me.

With what felt like a massive effort, she used the nearby crates to pull herself to her feet. She was shaking, perhaps through weakness, or perhaps because of adrenaline, but either way she would have to force herself to walk, to run if necessary. Malcolm was upstairs, she could sense him, and she needed to get to him somehow. She clung to the wall, the shelves, the various items strewn about the room, using them as perches to keep her going, slowly making her way toward the bottom of the steps. She could feel the warmth of blood making its way down her legs. He hadn't got around to raping her just yet, instead he had been using a flick knife he kept inside his shirt pocket to cut her inner thigh and genitals. She wasn't sure how much damage he had done, but she was beginning to feel light headed from the loss of blood. As she reached the steps, clutching to the bannister, she looked back to see a trail of blood, her red footprints clearly marking her unsteady route through the room. She looked down and saw that what she thought had been a trickle was in fact a steady flow, and she understood the extent of what he had done to her. She wondered why it didn't hurt more, why there was only a dull ache. Perhaps I'm already dead.

The door above her opened with such force it reverberated as it hit the wall behind it. She expected to see Savage, but instead there was a man she had not seen before. He was tall and black, with wide, broad shoulders straining to escape from his once white V neck t-shirt, a red stain spreading across it now like ink on a page. His eyes were wide with fear, and he clutched at his stomach, moaning. He tried to take a step, but tumbled down the stairs, landing at her feet with a thud. He rolled onto his back, still clutching his stomach, his breathing short and sharp, his eyes darting around wildly. When he saw her watching him, he focused on her and raised his hand towards her, drops of blood falling from his outstretched fingers onto the concrete below. A moment later, his hand fell as he let out a sigh, and he was dead. His eyes were fixed on hers still, the whites bright in the darkness as they reflected the light from the open door above them.

Apart from her Grandmother, she had never really seen a dead body before. Yes, she had watched Mickey as he passed, but she'd passed out so quickly, she had only seen him there a moment. As she stared down at the face of a young man no older than nineteen, a boy really, she thought she would feel something, compassion maybe, or perhaps disgust or something close to sadness. Instead when she looked down at the lifeless face of one of her captors, she felt almost pleased. She was glad he was dead, and as she began to drag herself up each step, she hoped with every fibre of her being that Savage would soon be next.

Fraser tried to get his breath back as they split up to search the rest of the building. He and Malcolm, and a muscular bald man Fraser recognised from the whiteboard in his office as being Brian Weir, aka 'Raging Bull', searched this floor. The mass who forced the door, whom Fraser decided to nickname 'The Wall', lead the rest of his goons up to search the two floors above. He didn't know why, but something told him she was beneath them, in the cellar below. It was as if he could sense her close by, and that closeness made it all the more nerve-wracking as adrenaline surged through his veins.

They checked what used to be the toilets, an overwhelming stench hitting their nostrils as soon as they opened the door. There was piss on the floor, and the smell of shit made him gag. Graffiti covered the walls, and as he checked the final stall, a large black spray painted skull stared back at him, red paint dripping from its gritted teeth. He shuddered slightly at the sight of it, its hollow eyes staring him down, staying with him even after he ran on to the next room.

As they made their way through the building, they encountered more of Savage's men. One or two held their hands above their heads the second they entered, only to be met with the butt of a shot gun in recognition of their surrender.

But, as they entered the final door, once a function room, all hell broke loose. As soon as the Bull kicked the door in, he took three shots to the chest, his blood hitting the side of Fraser's face as he leapt behind a nearby games machine. Bullets sprayed around him, the wall behind bursting into fireworks of dust and plaster, the machine spilling the change inside onto the floor after taking another shot, as if it too was wounded. He could see the pump action shotgun which the Wall had been using lying beside his now limp and lifeless arm. Malcolm was still outside the room, taking shots around the doorway before moving back into cover to reload. Fraser signalled him and pointed at the shotgun on the floor.

Malcom nodded in understanding as he began to shoot every bullet in the magazine at the bar ahead, covering Fraser long enough to seize the gun and duck back into cover.

He hadn't wanted to kill anyone, but he was left with no option. The gun weighed heavily in his hands. This was the only way now. Malcolm edged slightly into his sight line and signalled to a large chest freezer at the other side of the door. Fraser nodded, stepping out and pumping three, four, five shots into the back of the bar. As shards of glass flew and wood splintered, Malcolm darted to the space just behind the freezer, and as soon as he was in, Fraser took position behind a stack of tables and chairs just beyond, hoping as he did so that there was enough of them piled up to provide protection from the bullets flying around him, and praying that the freezer Malcolm crouched behind didn't contain the woman he loved.

The shard of light edging through the half-opened door above acted as a beacon as she ascended the stairs. She wondered if this was what it was like to die, edging towards a bright light above, but the aching in her thighs, the pain of every step taken, was a reminder that she was alive, at least for now. The closer she got, the louder the sounds of gunfire and yelling became. She began to make out words, and tone, and she could sense the panic of the men she could hear, their voices raised and desperate. The smell too had begun to change as she got closer to the door. Gone was the mustiness, the dampness of her prison, replaced with the unmistakable smell of gun oil, and something else, the coppery smell of blood and death.

She peered around the edge of the door frame, careful to stay hidden. The light, despite being inside, was brighter than anything she'd ever encountered before, and for a moment it blinded her, white and black spots swimming across her vision like giant creatures in an alien world. She held tightly to the frame, splinters forcing their way into her palms as she tried to keep her balance. Slowly, her vision returned. She was in the far corner of what appeared to have once been a pub of some kind. The red wallpaper, peeling in swathes, washed the room in an ominous red glow, the only light coming from a dirty skylight overhead, caked by years of bird shit and London soot.

The carpet beneath her feet was damp and mouldy, but she welcomed the feel of something soft after the concrete. The door opposite had a crooked 'WC' sign on it, to her left was a swing door with 'Bar' once painted gold, but now fading into the wood. Through it she could hear the shouting, the bangs and pops of gun fire, and the cries of dying men.

To her right was a heavy exit door wedged open by an old, rusted fire extinguisher, its contents long since spent. She could feel the breeze through the opening, fresh air tempting her, pulling her to the outside, to freedom. It took her full weight, but the door slowly edged open on its rusted hinges, revealing a small enclosed yard. A further door beyond which must have lead onto the street or an alleyway had a collection of rusted padlocks hanging from it, making the large new one appear all the shinier by comparison. It was the only new thing she'd seen since being taken to this place, the dust and the damp having claimed it decades before.

She put her hand out first. It was raining lightly, and even through caked in dirt and dry blood, she could feel the cold drops of water hitting her palm and edging their way slowly along her hand, following the path etched there by her lifelines. She smiled for the first time in days. She had never liked the rain. She always associated it with days unable to play outside, with ruining outfits or hair styles or summer plans, with sadness. But now, in that moment, she loved it, appreciating its life-giving properties for the first time as it revived and awakened her. She wanted so badly to run out into it, to hold her mouth open as a child would, and drink. Perhaps she could use the crates and tables lying rotting around the yard as a platform from which to scale the wall, or break the padlock with the extinguisher and escape this hell. But she couldn't, not yet. Somewhere inside, Malcolm was fighting for her life, perhaps for his own too, and she wouldn't abandon him.

Then there was Savage. Everything he'd done to her began to spread and swell inside her, like the waves of the ocean ebbing ever closer, claiming more and more of the beach as they go. If she didn't end this here and now, he would forever haunt her. The boogeyman of her nightmares, the shadow in her peripheral vison. She refused to live a life of fear, always looking over her shoulder. More than that, she knew this was not his first time inflicting torture and it would certainly not be his last, he loved it too much. That had been obvious by the look in his eyes as he hurt her, as he violated her. She would not let this happen to another woman. Never again. He has to be stopped.

Reluctantly, she turned back, and using the wall to steady herself, made her way down the short, narrow corridor towards the door ahead. Only now did she notice the red bloodied handprints following her path but leading their way in the opposite direction towards the basement door, their owner lifeless at the bottom of the stairs. Without realizing, she placed her hand in his palm print, almost exactly lining up together. Although his fingers were much longer, his palm much larger, she could clearly see the lines and marks which mapped out his short life, and she noticed how little they differed from hers, both sets of swirls melting into the other in the still wet blood.

As she reached the door, she peered through a gap created along the edge by damp rotting wood after years of use. The door opened just beside the bar, a large wooden relic of a past life. It was opened at the side, and behind the dusty shelves, she could make out a figure darting back and forth into view, shooting around the edge of or above the bar before returning behind the safety its thick frame provided. She could hear the figure yelling to other voices, sometimes seeing arms or guns coming into view. She guessed there were three or four of them, but couldn't be sure.

Beyond the bar itself, she could see into a large room, it's dull, misty light revealing furniture stacked, an old chest freezer with brown stains slowly destroying its once white body, broken gambling machines, and piles of rubble and rubbish. In its current state, it was difficult to picture what it had looked like in its heyday. On the walls of the corridor were a couple of old sepia-coloured photographs, the smiling faces of people staring back at her through time. The nearest was a wedding, and guessing by the style of dress, it must have been the sixties. All of the people raised their glasses to her, and the bride smiled proudly, holding her groom's hand. She remembered her own wedding day, her own smiling face, and she wondered where this couple was now, if they were even still alive. She wondered if they had a happy marriage, if they'd been content with their choice right until the end?

A loud gunshot coming from inside the hall brought her back from the past, from a room once used to make such happy memories, now awash with blood and death. She heard the pump of a shotgun, followed by another shot, repeating again and again. She pushed the door slightly, keeping low and out of sight, to see who was firing. That was when she saw them.

Fraser stood almost in the exact centre of the room, a shotgun held in both hands, firing repeatedly towards the bar. She could hear wood splintering, glass breaking, men yelling as they ducked for cover. He was bleeding, and even in the dull light she could see the purple of a bruise circling his left eye. As he fired, another figure darted from the open door beyond, dashing for the chest freezer. Even though the figure was blurred and hunched, she could immediately tell who it was and she felt hope for the first time in days. Malcolm.

They were pinned down and outnumbered, Fraser knew that as he huddled behind the chairs, the room awash with dust, like a fog refusing to settle. For the first time, he wished Malcolm's men were there, and wondered what was taking those who had gone upstairs so long to come back. Maybe they were dead. For their sakes he hoped not. He had a look at the shotgun in his hands, the weight increasing with every second. He had one more shell. He glanced at Malcolm, and watched him do the same as he removed the mag of his Glock to examine the contents inside. He signalled to Fraser with two fingers. Three shots. That was all they had. He wanted to scream in frustration. He was so near to her; he could feel it. They couldn't stop now. Not when they were so close.

Marie checked the toilets for a weapon, but apart from the rusted fire extinguisher, she had nothing. I have to do something. I have to help them. She stumbled outside again, the drizzle now a heavy rain, the water pooling in the centre of the yard. She frantically searched through the rubbish, the remnants of the building's past, for something, for anything. She almost tripped over it, the rusted square can, its contents sloshing inside as it fell to the ground. She recognised the old label almost immediately from her Grandmother's room. Memories of being held by her during blackouts, a regular occurrence in a household where much of the money meant for bills was regularly drunk, the gentle light it created warming the dark room with its comforting glow as her Grandmother sang to her. It was kerosene.

She picked it up and could feel it was at least half full. She ran towards the noise and blood and darted down the stairs of the cellar, back into her prison. Back into that darkness. She fell to the ground beside his body, hitting the concrete hard, a sharp pain shooting up through her knees. She ignored it, searching his pockets, praying he was a smoker, his eyes still frozen and wide with fear. When she felt the smooth, cool metal of the lighter in his jeans, she almost cried out. She pulled it out and surveyed her prize; a gold zippo with an engraving obscured by the blood of its owner. She wiped it and read the inscription, 'Happy 18th love Mum.'

It took more effort to stand than it had to kneel, but soon she was running up the stairs, the kerosene in one hand, the lighter in the other. When she got to the top of the stairs, she realised the shots had stopped, replaced with yelling. She stopped dead when she heard him, his voice forever engrained on her mind, the voice of her captor. She could only just make out the words, but it was the tone that brought that now familiar dread to her. It was mocking, it was almost jovial. He was taunting them. It was then she realised Fraser and Malcolm were in real trouble.

Fraser couldn't decide which was worse; shots being fired or the silence that suddenly filled the room. They were too low on ammunition to continue forward, and Savage was either in the same position, or he knew they were pinned down. He could hear shots echoing from upstairs, of running footsteps and heavy thuds above, and he suddenly realised why their backup wasn't there.

A high pitched laugh pierced through the silence. It was the laugh of someone unhinged, but worse, it was the genuine, hearty laugh of someone who found actual joy in this situation. He felt his jaw clench, the taste of blood increasing as he did so. He knew who owned that laugh, and he was filled with a sudden surge of loathing. Every fibre of his being wanted to run towards it, to beat that laugh into silence again, to wipe the smile of the smug face of its owner, but he knew that would be suicide.

"Well boys, we seem to have ourselves a bit of a Mexican stand off on our hands. There's a lot less shooting coming from your side, which gets me thinking you might be low on ammunition, maybe even out. Am I right boys?" That laugh again, this time louder, accompanied by the sound of a gun cocking. "See, this shithole here is my shithole, and I happen to have a fuckload of guns and ammo in it. On top of that, you boys seem to be on your own now, while I have three of my biggest, baddest friends back here with me, and God knows how many kicking the ass of your mates upstairs. You're outmanned and outgunned boys. Basically, you're fucked."

There was other laughter now, not just his, and although it was less sure, it still sent a shiver down Fraser's spine. The realisation that they really were cornered began to set in, and for the first time he thought about what that would mean. His body would be found, in pieces most likely, another unsolved murder on the ever growing pile at his office. He thought about his Father, about the family he didn't have, that he most likely would never have now, and he felt the weight of more than three decades of regret weighing down on him. He thought of Marie, of letting her down. Maybe she was already dead. Maybe this whole thing was for nothing? Maybe he betrayed everything he stood for, his job, his integrity, and it was all for nought. He felt tears well up in his eyes. He looked at Malcolm and realised he had the same look on his face.

Marie placed the can against the door and allowed a small trickle to slowly make its way under, snaking towards the bar and the source of the cackling. It was easier than she thought, the floor was concrete and must have been on a slight slope, the path of the kerosene running smoothly towards the wood of the bar, pooling on the floor before edging its way along out of her sight. When the weight of the can began to feel light in her hands, the liquid assassin leaving the place it had called home for so many years, the smell of it increasing, she held the lighter out, careful to keep it just below the steady flow. She tried it once, twice, but only a dull glow appeared, a flame refusing to manifest. Panic arose in her throat as she listened to him taunting them, telling them they were going to die, and she found herself praying. It lit on the third attempt, the liquid igniting immediately and spreading out in a river of flames.

The screaming was almost instantaneous. A figure appeared from behind the bar, scrambling to put out the flames spreading up his legs, licking at his waist, before a single shot pierced his screams, suddenly ending them as he fell to the ground, the flames claiming his body as their spoils. She didn't even hesitate, as she pushed open the bar door and lunged onto the nearest figure fighting to extinguish the flames with his hoody whilst trying his best to remain hidden behind the bar. She had taken him by surprise and he fell forwards with a thud, his head splitting against the corner of the bar.

She went to pull the gun from his limp hand, but another figure hit her hard across the face. As she fell backwards, she was sure this was it, that she was about to die, but from behind she heard the pump of a shotgun before a wash of red exploded across her attacker's chest and he fell backwards with the force. She looked back in time to see Fraser get hit on the shoulder and stumble backwards. She felt grief surge through her as she let out a scream, the fear for Fraser's life far outweighing the fear for her own.

The flames were dying now and the smell of burned flesh and wood filled the room. Smoke drifted around them creating the impression of a fog, and for a second Marie saw her home in Northern Ireland, on a cool misty day, and she wished she was back there for the first time since she had fled.

Fraser didn't think, he had just acted. As soon as the flames appeared, he knew it was her. He knew she was alive, and that she was fighting to get to him. A scream had pierced the room, a stark contrast from the manic laughter, and a man stood up from behind the bar hitting at his feet as they were engulfed in flame. Malcolm hadn't hesitated, rising from behind the freezer and sending off a perfectly aimed shot, hitting the man almost between the eyes. He fell to the ground with a thud, the flames now unheeded spreading over him in a wave.

It was hard to make out the bar now, as the flames licked at damp wood in a futile attempt to continue to live. The smoke it created was so heavy it appeared as if it rose with great effort. Even through the grey curtain it created, he could see her barrel through the door. Without hesitation, he found himself running towards her. He didn't care if this was the last thing he ever did, he had to save her. He got the shot off just in time, sending the figure flying backwards. A split second later he felt the pain surge through his right shoulder as he was knocked in the opposite direction. He thought he heard a scream, but it seemed like it was far away, as if the force of the bullet had somehow thrown him down a long tunnel.

The pain was worse than anything he'd ever experienced. It spread through his chest along with the warm dampness of his blood. He had no shots left. There was nothing he could do now. He looked at Marie, her face contorted with fear, and reached out to her. If he was going to die, he wanted to die near her.

The gun lay free now, but before she had time to pick it up another shot came from behind her. She must have moved just in time, the bullet carving its way across the surface of her arm as it flew past. She cried out, her hand failing her as she continued to scramble for the weapon.

There was another shot. She closed her eyes for a moment, convinced the target was her, waiting for the pain, the blood. But she wasn't hit, she was alive. She opened her eyes just in time to see a figure falling towards her, but not in time to avoid him as he landed, the weight of the impact winding her. She scrambled to get out from under him, his lolling head and lifeless eyes right by hers, as if death itself was contagious.

When Malcolm came around the side of the bar, the mahogany now peppered with bullet holes, he held his gun aloft, pointing it at the only remaining threat behind that bar, Jonathan Savage. Only Fraser knew, and no doubt Malcolm was also painfully aware, that the gun was now empty, as was his own. If Savage continued to resist, decided to go down with his ship, they had no way to stop him.

Marie moved towards him, and pressed the wound on his shoulder. He could see she was covered in blood, both old and new, and he wanted so desperately to fix it, to fix everything she had been through. He placed his hand on hers and they looked at each other a moment, a silent message passing between them both. I wish things could have been different.

"Drop the gun, Savage. It's over. Your men are dead. Your empire is dead. Drop the gun or you'll join them."

That laugh again. This time it didn't sound so genuine, so cocky. It sounded like the noise a trapped animal would make, the sound of a desperate man in his final moments.

Fraser could see him through the gloom, a silhouette illuminated by the dying flames. He was holding something. Something long. It was a shotgun. "Maybe this film could end like one of those old westerns? We count to ten and draw, see who wins? Sounds like fun to me."

"My gun's already raised and pointed directly at your head. You've seen how good a shot I am. You'd never have a chance."

"See, here's the thing Mal, I can call you Mal right? I'm starting to wonder if you have any bullets left in that gun of yours. Seems to me, and I may be way off here, but I would have expected you to shoot me by now. The whole not being shot part makes me suspect your bluffing. Are you bluffing?"

Fraser felt his heart beat faster and faster inside his chest. The kid was right and they knew it. Poker was obviously Savage's game.

"The man behind me is a cop. He made me promise not to kill anyone unless it was in self-defense. I'm a man of my word."

Savage laughed again, tapping the side of the shotgun on the side of his leg, like a kid with ADHD. "Let's see if that's true shall we?"

Marie breathed Fraser in, and for a moment she imagined what her life would have been like if she had married someone like him. Someone safe. She held him a moment, trying to pretend, just for a second, that this wasn't real. That Fraser and her were just at their home, cuddling on their Homebase sofa, watching a police comedy on their big screen TV. But that wasn't the life she had chosen. And even the dream seemed wrong to her, like she was trying to place herself into a situation in which she didn't belong, like forcing two mismatched jigsaw puzzle pieces together. She cared for Fraser, yes, but she didn't love him. Not like that. That fantasy would remain just that, a fantasy.

Everything was tense. Only moments before, the noise had been deafening, but now you could hear everyone breathing heavily, the only other noise the crackle of dying flames. Both men refused to bend, both refused to break, and it could only end one way.

Marie moved the gun she'd been reaching for towards her with her foot, gripping it tightly when it was within reach. Neither of the men above her seemed to notice, they were too focused on each other, tunnel vision setting in. Malcom may have made a promise to Fraser, but she hadn't. After everything he had done, he deserved to die, and she wanted to be the one to kill him.

"Do you know what I did to her? Do you know what I did to your sweet little Marie?"

She felt Fraser tense beside her, and saw Malcolm squeeze the gun in his hands, his grip shifting and tightening at the mention of her name. "Oh we had some fun, me and her. She tastes like cherries, so sweet. And that pussy of hers, that was one of the tightest little cunts I ever had the pleasure of fucking."

"Shut the fuck up!" Malcolm had lost all of the calm in his voice. He sounded angry, and devastated, and afraid. He sounded afraid. It was then that she realised there were no bullets in that gun, that Malcolm was defenseless. She didn't hesitate.

"I knew you were bluff..."

The first shot ripped through his side, forcing him back into the bar. He tried to raise the gun, but the second shot tore through his shin, splintering bone and sinew as it went, and he crumpled to the floor screaming out in pain as he fell.

Malcolm lunged, grabbing the gun from beside him before Savage had a chance to act. He pointed it at his head and pulled the trigger, but the gun simply clicked. It was empty. He smacked Savage with the butt of the gun over and over, getting five, six, seven blows in before Marie was beside him, holding him. He dropped the gun and held her.

They stayed like that for some time. Savage moaning beside them, Marie and Malcolm crying with relief, never saying a word, with hurried kisses, reunited. And as Fraser watched on, for a moment he thought he could feel his heart actually breaking.

They were interrupted by the sound of approaching footsteps, of voices getting louder, moving towards them. Malcolm took the gun from Marie and stood up to face the door, the gun raised, his hands shaking slightly. He didn't even know if it was loaded.

The voices grew louder, and Malcolm gripped the barrel tighter, while Marie searched behind the bar for ammunition, a weapon, something. He almost fired a shot when his man entered.

"Whoa whoa boss, it's us."

Three men entered the room, one being helped along by another, a red blood stain visible on the leg of his jeans. Fraser recognised the first one as the man he nicknamed 'The Wall', his face now swollen and sweaty. They were breathing heavily, and had obviously been involved in one hell of a fight. Fraser wondered what exactly had gone on upstairs, and just as quickly realised he would rather not know. The body count was already worryingly high.

They had won. Malcolm had won, the turf war was over, but at what cost? Fraser closed his eyes tightly, the pain that had been throbbing was slowly becoming a dull ache. He had no idea what to do next, how to explain any of this, the bullet hole in his shoulder, the bodies, the blood. His career would be over, his job had been everything to him, it had been who he was, until he met her. Until Marie.

His thoughts were interrupted by the howls of pain, a foot stomping on a shattered, bloodied leg, a fist breaking ribs. Malcolm was going to town on Savage. That gentleman criminal act had well and truly gone now, the rage and grief overriding every other thought and emotion. He was going to beat him to death, the look on his face made that clear. He wouldn't stop until he was pounding red goo into the cracks in the floor.

Fraser dragged himself up with great effort, bear hugging Malcolm from behind. It wasn't easy, his shoulder felt like it was trying to separate itself from his body, and the rage Malcolm felt had given him an almost inhuman strength, but he held him as tightly as he could, barely holding him back from Savage's whimpering form.

"If you do this, you're no better than him, you hear me? Stop." He could hear the men approach him from the other side of the room, the clodding footsteps of the Wall unmistakable as they made their way towards him. He braced himself for a fight.

"Don't."

It was Marie. The footsteps stopped immediately, and Malcolm went limp in Fraser's arms. In that moment he truly understood just how much

Malcolm loved Marie, a single word from her enough to kill that rage dead, that rage that only seconds before had been beating another human being to a pulp. She had a hold on him, on both of them.

She cupped Malcolm's face in her hands and wiped the tears from his cheeks before kissing him gently. Fraser was still holding him, no longer in an effort to keep him back, but merely to keep him upright, his body almost a dead weight. She looked at him then, and he thought she understood, that she agreed with him, she was in tune with him. There had been enough blood shed. It was over now.

But then her face changed, her eyes darkened, and for a moment he didn't recognise her. "You don't have to protect me anymore. This isn't your job Malcolm. It's mine."

He didn't understand, not until he saw the knife in her hand.

"Marie, don't..."

Malcolm shifted almost instantly, his full strength was now against Fraser, he was now holding Fraser back, he was the calm one now.

"After what he did to me?"

"There's been enough death, enough blood. Let me take him in. Let me do this properly."

"He needs to be punished."

"You're right, you're absolutely right. But not like this. He should go to court, to prison. He should rot in a cell. He's hurt a lot of people, and they all deserve justice."

"Justice? Ha."

He stopped pushing against Malcolm now. Her voice seemed so cold, so detached. That wasn't her, that wasn't his Marie.

"Do you really think that would happen Fraser? Look at him. Look at this place. How would you explain this to your bosses, to the courts? You chose to do this our way, and it's going to end our way."

"Our way? Marie..." He trailed off, he didn't know what to say, what to do. She was right of course. How could this be done legally now? There were a dozen bodies, a hole clean through his shoulder, a suspect shot and beaten. If anyone would end up in jail, it was him. But the part of him that believed in good, in right, was still crying out inside his head. The other deaths weren't in cold blood; they were self-defense. They had been attacked, it was kill or be killed. This, this was different. This was a defenseless, injured, unarmed man. This was murder, plain and simple. No matter what Savage had done, this wasn't right.

"Yes, Fraser, our way. I told you before, I'm not some damsel in distress. I've made my choices; I know who I am. I'm not who you think I am. Maybe I never was."

"He isn't a threat anymore. This isn't self-defense, this isn't justice, it's cold blooded murder."

"Maybe. But it's what he deserves." Marie turned the knife over in her hands, the handle felt cold against her palms, and there was something comforting in its weight. She had removed it from Malcolm's pocket when she kissed him. He allowed her to take it, he had looked at her with understanding. He knew what she was feeling, because he felt it too, the grief, the anger, the hatred. But he was willing to set his aside, to give her what she needed, to allow her the chance to take back everything that Savage had stripped from her. Blood for blood.

She looked at Fraser, his face awash with helplessness and confusion. Part of her wished she was the person he thought she was; that the Marie he had envisaged in her could somehow manifest itself, but that wasn't her. Perhaps, if things had been different, that's who she would have been. But there was no point dwelling on what ifs, not anymore. She was who she was, and Fraser needed to see that for himself.

She turned towards Savage and plunged the knife into his crotch, twisting it as he screamed helplessly. She leant down to his ear, barely distinguishable amongst the blood and mangled flesh of his swollen face, and whispered to him. "How does it feel? To have something forced inside you, to be violated? Do you like it Savage? Do you?"

She was surprised at how easy it was to inflict pain on another human being, at how satisfying revenge felt. She wanted him to die, but not yet. A quick death was too good for him.

She pulled the knife out, the fresh blood warm on her hand, and walked past Fraser and Malcolm. She gave the knife to The Wall, pressing the handle into his hand as if to emphasise her point. "Make it last as long as possible, do you understand? Keep him alive as long as you can, get a nurse if you have to, I don't care. Just make sure it's slow and painful and lasts for days."

"Yes boss."

She went to Malcolm and held his hand tight in

hers. She wanted to get out of that hell hole. She wanted to wash and sleep, but mostly she wanted to be with Malcolm, to breathe him in, to be safe in his arms. His boys could clear this up, she was done with it.

She looked at Fraser, a tear etching its way down his cheek, a look of devastation on his face. She understood the grief he now felt. He was mourning the loss of a love he had just this second realised he never had, the loss of a woman who had never existed. He had painted an image in his mind of her before they had even crossed paths, and she would never have lived up to it. He knew it now, how foolish he had been, how naïve. She wished she could comfort him, but it was too late now. It was better this way; better he knew for certain so he could move on.

"Go home, Fraser. Go home."

Epilogue

Marie stared out of the small, characterless window into the Police Station car park while she waited for the officer to arrive for their appointment. It was another dull, rainy day outside and she struggled to recall the sun ever shining whilst she was inside this building. The stark grey walls appeared even drearier under a grey sky. But perhaps that was appropriate, she thought. After all, people never came to Police Stations for a happy reason. You either worked here, which was bound to be stressful and depressing, you were the victim of a crime, or a suspect being dragged kicking and screaming into a custody cell. Yes, it suits the grey.

The door opened behind her and she heard a man with a posh English accent apologise for being late. She didn't turn around immediately, half expecting it to be him, to be Fraser, perhaps hoping it would be. But it wouldn't be, she knew that. She had enquired a month or so after the bar, had someone look into him, to see how he was doing. Partly, she wanted to make sure he had been sensible enough to keep what happened to himself, but she knew he would. If not for his career, he would have kept it secret out of shame. Shame for betraying his job, his conscience, who he was and what he stood for, and shame for being so foolish, for being so wrong about her, about everything. And perhaps she thought a small part of him would keep it secret for her, to keep her safe one last time. But mostly, she had wanted to make sure he was okay. She felt shame too, for leaving him like she had, standing in that bar, after everything he had given up to save her. And despite everything, she cared about him deeply.

He had transferred back to Scotland. She hoped distance would be enough for him to heal. There had never been any suspicion against him, Malcolm and she had made sure of it. The bodies had disappeared, Savage simply disappeared, the bar burned to the ground. No witnesses came forward; if there were any, they knew better. The amount of murder investigations went down, just as the amount of missing persons suddenly spiked, a gang of criminals with several kids each to several different mothers, seemingly disappeared into thin air. Questions were asked, cases ran cold, and whilst some officers had strong suspicions, no one could ever prove anything. And eventually, one case was replaced by another, and another, newspapers had new celebrity scandals and stories of Police ineptitude and rising crime stats to report on, and everything was forgotten. Except by them. They would never forget.

"Please take a seat, Mrs. Carter."

He was black, in his mid-fifties perhaps, grey lines dappling his once jet black hair. He wore a pale pink shirt with a grey tie. He was very neat, very together. The files in front of him were neatly stacked, and the three pens in his shirt pocket were all identical, all pointing the same way. He had a warm face, there was something fatherly about him.

She pulled the heavy chair out from the table, the chains connecting it to the floor jangling slightly as she did so, and sat down directly facing the Detective. He opened a file and began to shuffle through the papers. She took the time to appraise him, like a competitor assessing her opponent. She knew what was to come. He seemed nervous, beads of sweat forming on his wrinkled brow, patches of darker pink visible under his arms. There was a gold band on his wedding finger, scratched and dented from years of wear. She wondered if he had any children, how old they were. Perhaps they weren't far off her in age.

After what seemed like several minutes, he looked up from the papers, and stared at her. He had dark brown eyes filled with experience. She knew this wasn't his first rodeo, yet she seemed to make him anxious. Perhaps he'd heard the rumours about her, about his predecessor in the investigation being involved in some disappearances, things that could never be proven but followed this case like a bad smell. Perhaps he was worried about his own career and how this case would change him. He looked like he didn't have long to go before retirement, perhaps he just wanted to go home to that family she imagined, and leave all this murder and evil behind for good.

"Would you like a cup of tea or coffee?"

"No thank you, I would just like to get this over with."

"Have you got somewhere to be, Mrs. Carter?"

"To be honest, Detective...?"

"Detective Walker, but please call me Fred."

"To be honest, Detective Walker, I would rather be anywhere than this place, so if you could just ask your questions."

He looked a little taken aback at her abruptness, but composed himself quickly, removing the first page from the folder in front of him. "Very well. Do you know this man?"

He set a picture in front of her. It was a mug shot of a younger Jonathan Savage, his eyes coldly staring into the camera, a wide grin on his face which didn't match his gaze. She felt the hairs rise on her neck, as if she had seen a ghost, but she didn't change her expression or allow her face to betray her emotions. She had learned how to compose herself, how to be unreadable. "I saw his picture on the news a while back, about those grisly murders and all those young men disappearing. I can't recall his name though, Smith or Sinclair or something."

"Savage. Jonathan Martin Savage."

"Yes that was it, Savage."

"But you never met him?"

"No." She swallowed hard. Even now, after all this time, she hated thinking about him, hated hearing his name.

"What about your husband? Does he know him?"

"That's something you'd have to ask him."

"What about these men?" He laid out photo after photo, all young men, all in tracksuits, some with neck tattoos, some in baseball caps. All of them smiling in their custody photos. She recognised a few from the bar, the fat one whose nose she had broken, the thin slimy one wearing the same hat she'd seen him in, the young black kid who had died beside her at the bottom of those stairs. The rest she presumed were the others who died that day, the ones who died afterwards when they asked too many questions or tried to take Savage's place, the ones who fled the city after their mates disappeared and their hangout burned down, fearing retribution from Malcolm, fearing they would join their friends. All of them smiling at her from the mug shots, as if this was just a big joke between them, a private joke the Detective wasn't in on.

She laughed, she couldn't help it. It was all so absurd, her being here, being asked the same questions, going through the same motions. After everything she had been through, everything she had seen, everything she had done, nothing had changed.

"Is something funny, Mrs. Carter? These boys, all of them, are missing, feared dead. And we think your husband had something to do with it."

He was angry now, raising his voice at her as she continued to laugh.

"Your husband is messed up in a lot of bad shit, Mrs. Carter. He's suspected of nearly two dozen murders including these boys, as well as a list of other charges as long as your arm. Do you even know who you're married to? What he's capable of."

She stopped laughing, sliding the photo of Savage from the pile. She stared into his eyes, hatred threatening to bubble to the surface. "We all are." She said it so quietly, he barely heard her. A whisper almost, a statement made as much to herself as to him.

"Excuse me?"

She looked at his wedding ring again, and wondered what he would do if the right pressure was applied, the right loved ones threatened. "We're all capable of it, Detective. Every last one of us."

Made in the USA
Columbia, SC
24 April 2018